THE PROPHET
FROM
EPHESUS

THE ROMAN MYSTERIES
by Caroline Lawrence

Also available:

—— A Roman Mystery ——

THE PROPHET
FROM EPHESUS

Caroline Lawrence

Orion
Children's Books

First published in Great Britain in 2009
by Orion Children's Books
a division of the Orion Publishing Group Ltd
Orion House
5 Upper St Martin's Lane
London WC2H 9EA
An Hachette Livre UK company

1 3 5 7 9 10 8 6 4 2

The Orion Publishing Group's policy is to use papers that
are natural, renewable and recyclable products and made
from wood grown in sustainable forests. The logging and
manufacturing processes are expected to conform to the
environmental regulations of the country of origin.

A catalogue record for this book is
available from the British Library

ISBN 978 1 84255 191 2

Typeset by Input Data Services Ltd,
Bridgwater, Somerset

Printed in Great Britain by Clays Ltd, St Ives plc

www.orionbooks.co.uk

To my grandsons, Adrian and Jasper,
and their mother Brooke

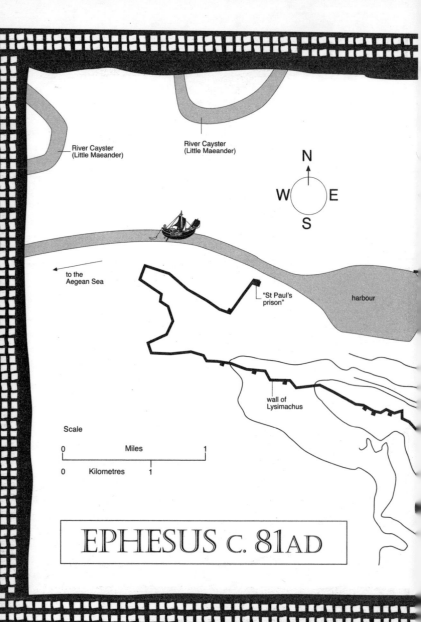

River Cayster
(Little Maeander)

River Cayster
(Little Maeander)

N
W E
S

to the
Aegean Sea

"St Paul's
prison"

harbour

wall of
Lysimachus

Scale

0 Miles 1

0 Kilometres 1

EPHESUS c. 81AD

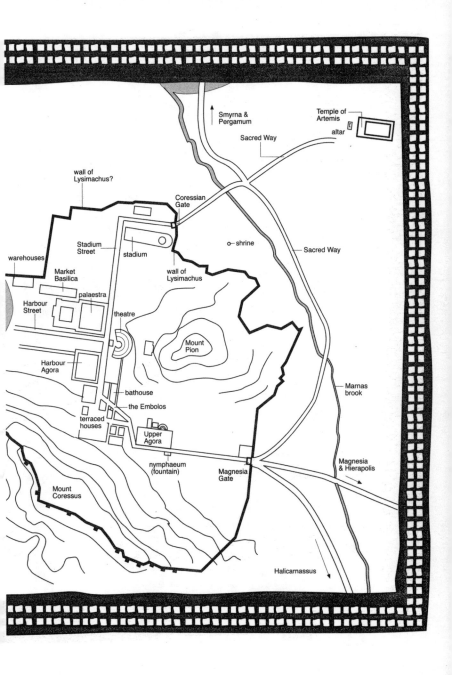

Smyrna &
Pergamum

Temple of
Artemis

altar

Sacred Way

wall of
Lysimachus?

Coressian
Gate

o— shrine

Sacred Way

Stadium
Street

stadium

warehouses

wall of
Lysimachus

Market
Basilica

palaestra

Harbour
Street

theatre

Mount
Pion

Marnas
brook

Harbour
Agora

bathouse

the Embolos

terraced
houses

Upper
Agora

nymphaeum
(fountain)

Magnesia
Gate

Magnesia
& Hierapolis

Mount
Coressus

Halicarnassus

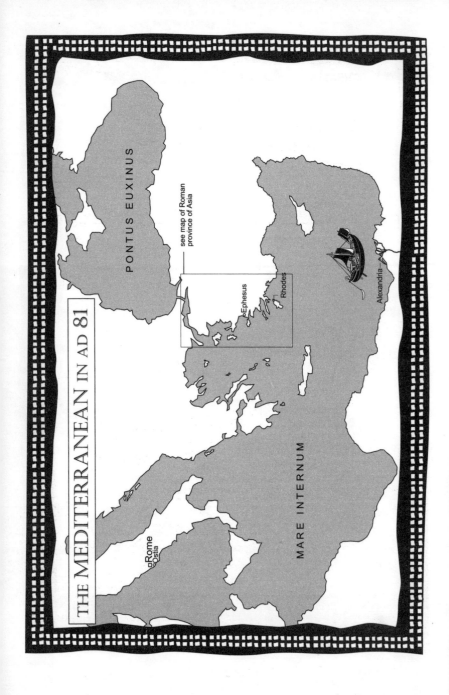

THE MEDITERRANEAN IN AD 81

PONTUS EUXINUS

MARE INTERNUM

Rome
Ostia

Ephesus

Rhodes

see map of Roman
province of Asia

Alexandria—A

This story takes place in ancient Roman times, so a few of the words may look strange.

If you don't know them, 'Aristo's Scroll' at the back of the book will tell you what they mean and how to pronounce them.

At the beginning of this book you will find a map of Turkey, which the Romans called Asia. Over two thousand years, some of the coastline has changed, so don't use this map to find your way around Turkey today! There is also a map of Ephesus as it was in the late first century AD, before some of its more famous monuments were built.

SCROLL I

In his vision he sees a celestial battle.

The sky is cobalt blue and full of stars. The whole of the Zodiac is there, as if inked in light on the inside of a vast bowl. The Maiden. The Lion. The Water-bearer. Stars pursue and confront each other with terrible purpose across this apocalyptic background.

He does not understand this terrifying conflict. All he knows is that there is a great battle and that the struggle is fiercest in the constellation of the Heavenly Twins, in the constellation of Gemini.

Flavia Gemina had a problem. She and her three friends were trapped in the city of Alexandria, a thousand miles from home.

'If we don't get out of this city and back to Ostia,' said Flavia one hot afternoon, 'I think I'll go mad.'

It was early August in the second year of the emperor Titus. For ten days the friends had been hiding out in a small house in the Rhakotis district of Alexandria, in the Roman province of Egypt. The house belonged to a newlywed couple honeymooning in Canopus. Their only contact to the outside world was the groom's cousin Nathan, a young Jewish boatman who had helped them in a quest up the Nile. He specialised in smuggling

I

goods in and out of Alexandria and at the moment he was trying to find a way to smuggle the four friends out of the city. In the meantime, they were confined to the first floor triclinium so that nobody would see them.

For the hundredth time, Flavia picked up the papyrus notice that Nathan had illegally pulled from a wall. Its message was in Greek:

Reward offered for four children: Jonathan son of Mordecai, aged twelve years: of medium height, olive skin, short curly hair, scar on left shoulder. Lupus or Lykos, aged ten: a tongue-less mute with no other visible blemishes. Nubia, aged about thirteen: a dark-skinned Nubian girl with eyes of an unusual golden brown colour. Flavia Gemina, daughter of Marcus Flavius Geminus, sea captain, aged twelve years: medium height, fair-skinned, grey eyes, no visible blemishes. Last seen in Ombos, in the Thebaid. N.B. The girls may be disguised as boys or eunuchs. 1000 drachmae per child for any information leading to their capture and arrest.

Flavia sighed, put down the notice and looked around the small triclinium at her three friends. Jonathan was sitting on the right-hand dining couch, absently cleaning his fingernails with a stylus. With his dark curly hair and olive skin, he perfectly matched the description on the notice. Dark-skinned, golden-eyed Nubia sat opposite Jonathan, on the left-hand couch. She was stroking a sleek grey cat. Lupus, the youngest of them, sat cross-legged on the cool tile floor; he was making idle marks on the wax tablet which was his main method of communication.

Flavia sighed again. 'Sometimes I wish I'd never become a detectrix,' she said. 'I wish I'd never solved the case of pater's missing signet ring two years ago. I wish we'd never caught the dog-killer in Ostia and the three assassins in Rome, or rescued the kidnapped children and tracked a criminal mastermind to Rhodes.'

'Why not?' asked Jonathan, without looking up from cleaning his nails.

'Because I became – *we* became such good detectives that the emperor sent us on that secret mission. But it went wrong and now we're hunted fugitives, a thousand miles from home.'

Jonathan nodded glumly. 'If only we hadn't written those letters home,' he said. 'They might have believed Nathan's story that we were eaten by crocodiles in Middle Egypt.'

'What letters?' Nubia looked up from the cat and frowned.

'Didn't we tell you?' said Flavia. 'Before he went out this morning, Nathan told us he thinks the officials must have intercepted one of the letters we sent home. That's how they know we're still alive. Nathan also said that he might not be able smuggle us out together. Because the notice gives such accurate descriptions of the four of us, we might have to split up.'

'No!' cried Nubia. 'We must not be divided. We are family. We must stay together.'

Jonathan gave a wry grin. 'Nathan's right. If we try to leave together, we'll probably attract more attention than a troupe of naked pantomime dancers.'

Lupus chuckled, and glanced up at Jonathan with bright green eyes.

'Of course,' added Jonathan. 'They'll probably catch us, even if we do split up.'

'Well,' said Flavia, 'if they're going to catch us anyway,

then I think Nubia's right. We should stay together. We may not be related, but we're family.' She gazed at her dark-skinned friend affectionately. 'After all, didn't we just travel seven hundred miles up the Nile to find you? It would be silly for us to separate again now.'

Nubia regarded them gravely. 'It is better to die together than to die alone,' she said.

Lupus grinned and wrote on his wax tablet: IS THERE A THIRD CHOICE?

'Yes!' cried Flavia. 'As soon as Nathan gets us out of this city, we can sail back to Italia. Then I'm going to marry Gaius Valerius Flaccus and be a good Roman matron and have lots of babies. And I vow I'll never try to solve another mystery again.'

'I seem to remember you took a vow never to marry,' said Jonathan drily. 'Now you're taking a vow to stop solving mysteries? Maybe you should take a vow not to take vows.'

Flavia gave him a rueful grin, and leaned closer to the sandalwood screen over the central couch on which she sat. The screen allowed the Etesian breeze to flow through, but it kept them hidden from curious eyes in the houses opposite or on the street below. Flavia put her eye right up to one of the lozenge-shaped chinks. She could feel the cool breeze and she could see the Pharos rising above the rooftops of Alexandria. The lighthouse marked the entrance to the great harbour.

'Oh! It's so frustrating!' she muttered. 'At this very moment ships are setting sail for home. If only we were on board one of them!'

'I'm afraid you won't be able to go home for a very long time,' said a familiar voice from the doorway.

They all turned to see a handsome young Greek with

curly hair the colour of bronze. It was their tutor Aristo, whom they had not seen in half a year.

'Aristo!' cried Flavia. She jumped off the dining couch and ran to hug him. 'Oh, praise Juno! It's so good to see you!'

Aristo laughed as Lupus and Jonathan rushed to greet him, too.

'What about you, Nubia?' said Aristo, as Jonathan stepped back. 'Don't I get a hug from you, too?'

Flavia and her friends turned to Nubia, just in time to see her fall back onto the cushioned divan in a swoon.

Nubia opened her eyes and gazed up into Aristo's wonderful face. His arms were around her and there was a look of tender concern in his long-lashed brown eyes. She reached up and touched his cheek, velvety with three day's growth of beard. She could smell the delicious scent of his body oil – a musky lavender – and she almost swooned again.

'Aristo?' she whispered. 'Is it really you?'

'Who else?' He showed perfect white teeth in a smile so beautiful it felt like a knife twisting in her heart. His smile faded and he looked at her with concern. 'Are you all right? Has someone hurt you?'

'No one has hurt me,' said Nubia, trying to sit up. The grey cat jumped down from the couch and stalked out of the room.

'Here, Nubia,' said Flavia. 'Rest on these cushions.'

Aristo helped her to lean back on a silk-covered bolster. 'Praise Apollo, I've found you,' he said, and looked around at the others. 'Praise Apollo!'

Nubia felt the knife twist in her heart again. Aristo

was as glad to see the others as he was to see her. He had only taken her in his arms because she had fainted like a foolish girl. His right hand had been holding her left elbow, now it moved away. Despite the heat of the day, her skin felt cold without his touch.

'How did you find us?' Flavia asked Aristo.

'I found him.' A young man came into the dining room with a tray of sweating copper beakers. He wore a white conical hat and a tunic which left both shoulders and part of his right breast uncovered. Nathan was the Jewish boatman and smuggler who had helped them in their quest up the Nile. 'Here, Nubia.' He extended the tray. 'Have some chilled posca. It's hot as Vulcan's furnace today. No wonder you fainted.'

'Thank you,' said Nubia. She handed a beaker to Aristo, then took another one for herself.

'I thought you were attending the Sabbath service,' said Jonathan to Nathan, as he took a cup of posca. 'At the synagogue. Remember? You promised your mother you were going to be an observant Jew?'

'I know. I did. I was.' Nathan placed the tray on a low table. 'But after the service ended I went down to the harbour to put the finishing touches to my plan. Old habits die hard,' he said, with a wink at Jonathan. 'Anyway, it's good I did. One of my friends told me about a young Greek fresh off the boat from Ostia. I'd told them to keep their ears open for anyone asking about you,' he explained. 'So I got to Aristo here as soon as I could, but I'm afraid he'd already spoken to some officials. And that means they'll be looking even harder for you.'

'I'm sorry,' said Aristo. 'I didn't know you were wanted here, too.'

'What do you mean: "wanted here, too"?' Flavia frowned at him.

'The four of you are wanted in Italia.'

'We are wanted in Italia?' said Nubia, her eyes never leaving Aristo's face.

He nodded. 'There are notices up in Ostia's forum, the marketplace and even above the fountain on Green Fountain Street. They're offering a thousand sesterces each for information leading to your capture. I don't know what you've done, but you can't go back there.'

The four friends stared at him. So did Nathan.

'I thought if I could just smuggle them out of Alexandria,' he said to Aristo, 'they'd be safe. I didn't realise they were wanted elsewhere.'

'I'm afraid so,' said Aristo. 'I suspect by now there are notices up all over the Empire.'

'Are you saying we can't go back to Italia?' said Flavia. 'We can't go home?'

'Not as long as Titus is emperor,' said Aristo grimly. 'And maybe never.'

SCROLL II

'We can't go home to Ostia!' cried Flavia. 'This is terrible.'

'Yes,' said Aristo grimly. 'What in Hades did you do to incur the emperor's wrath?'

'Nothing!'

'Just stole an emerald from the governor of Mauretania,' said Jonathan, moodily sipping his posca.

'What?'

Flavia glared at Jonathan. 'It wasn't like that,' she said. 'Titus asked us to recover—'

'Emperor Titus?' said Aristo. 'The emperor himself asked you to do something?'

'Yes. He asked us to recover a gem which had originally belonged to him, an emerald called "Nero's Eye". So we did.'

'We didn't recover it,' said Jonathan. 'We stole it.'

'But it originally belonged to him,' said Flavia.

Aristo frowned. 'But why would the emperor send children on such an important and dangerous mission? Especially when he has his choice of agents and spies?'

Jonathan answered. 'He said children can go places where adults can't, and that we'd proved ourselves to him before.'

Lupus held up his wax tablet: SAID HE COULD TRUST US

'And you succeeded in the mission?' said Aristo.

'Yes,' said Flavia. 'We stole the emerald and we gave it to one of Titus's agents, a man named Taurus from Sabratha.'

'We think that was our mistake,' sighed Jonathan. 'We should have personally handed the gem to Titus. He obviously never got it and he probably thinks we kept it for ourselves.'

Flavia nodded. 'We think Taurus kept the gem for himself and put the blame on us. Anyway, we were on our way back to Italia when our ship was blown off course and ran aground. Lupus and Jonathan and I washed up together but we couldn't find Nubia. Then we discovered she was going up the Nile. We were following her when we discovered that some Egyptian officials were after us. They had a warrant for our arrest. It had come via Sabratha, where Titus's agent Taurus lived. Later we saw Taurus's slave with the officials.'

'That's how we know he betrayed us,' said Jonathan.

'Yes,' said Flavia. 'Nathan helped us trick the Egyptians into thinking we were dead, but when we got back here to Alexandria we found there were new notices up for our arrest.'

Jonathan added: 'We think they must have intercepted two letters we sent home, to tell you we were safe.'

'By all the gods,' muttered Aristo. 'And now there are notices up in Rome and Ostia, too.'

'Are they like this one?' Flavia handed Aristo the piece of papyrus.

He took it and nodded. 'Yes. Except the ones in Ostia are written in Latin and dated a week before the Kalends of August,' he said. 'Oh, and they have a small addition: they say you're wanted for treason against the Emperor.'

'Treason!' breathed Flavia. 'That means they can execute us if they find us.'

She stared at her friends in dismay.

Aristo shook his head. 'I'm afraid I'm the bearer of even more bad news.'

'More bad news?' cried Flavia. 'What could be worse than a charge of treason?'

Aristo put his beaker down on the table. 'Suppressio,' he said. 'The kidnapping of freeborn children.'

'We're accused of kidnapping?'

'No. There have been some more kidnappings. In Ostia.'

'Slave-dealers?' asked Flavia.

'Pirates?' whispered Nubia.

'Who?' asked Jonathan. 'Who was kidnapped?'

'Half a dozen freeborn children,' said Aristo, 'including Popo.'

'Alas!' cried Nubia.

Jonathan rested his head in his hands.

'Who's Popo?' asked Nathan, looking from one to the other.

Flavia explained: 'Last year,' she said, 'Jonathan's sister had twin boys, Philadelphus and Soter. Everybody calls them Popo and Soso.'

'How did it happen?' asked Jonathan, without raising his head from his hands.

'Popo was with one of his wet-nurses in the fish-market,' said Aristo, 'and they were both seized.'

'Why take Popo?' asked Jonathan. 'He's just a baby.'

'Six other freeborn children were taken the day

before,' said Aristo. 'The kidnappers must have done one last sweep. Your baby nephew was just in the wrong place at the wrong time. They took the girl, too.'

'Alas!' cried Nubia again, and Lupus growled.

'Who did it?' asked Flavia. 'Do they know?'

Aristo nodded. 'A youth came to the house a few hours after their abduction and told us he recognised the men who took them. His description fit with sightings of the kidnappers we had the day before. A mother of one of the other kidnapped children thinks they were from Rhodes.'

'But it can't be!' cried Flavia. 'We broke the slave-trade in Rhodes last year.'

'Your father thought that, too,' said Aristo to Flavia, 'But now he suspects that some of the Rhodians moved over to the mainland and have been operating from a base there.'

Flavia nodded. 'Gaius Valerius Flaccus went to Halicarnassus last year to try to find the leader of the kidnapping ring. We called him Biggest Buyer.'

'That's right. And now your father has gone there, too, in search of Popo and his wet-nurse. That's why he doesn't know you're alive.'

'Pater doesn't know we're alive?' said Flavia.

'No,' said Aristo. 'Your father thinks you're dead.'

Jonathan rested his head in his hands again. He felt sick. He knew this was all his fault.

He heard Flavia's voice saying, 'Pater thinks we're dead?'

'We all thought you were dead,' said Aristo. 'Your father returned from his voyage on the Kalends of June. He was nearly out of his mind when he discovered that the four of you had left Ostia back in March and were still missing three months later.'

'Oh, poor pater!' whispered Flavia. 'We were supposed to be back before him.'

'After several days of frantic investigation,' said Aristo, 'he realised you had gone to Sabratha. He was about to set sail to look for you when word reached us that the four of you were dead.'

'The shipwreck,' muttered Jonathan.

'Yes,' said Aristo. 'Ostia's harbourmaster received a report that the merchant ship *Tyche* had sunk. One of its crewmembers, a Phoenician, was picked up by a big grain ship on its way to Italia. He was floating on a piece of wreckage, and unconscious. When he recovered, he said there had been four Roman children aboard his ship, travelling with their uncle. The Phoenician believed he was the only survivor.'

'Uncle Gaius hasn't come home, has he?' asked Flavia.

'I'm afraid not.'

'Alas!' whispered Nubia. 'Marcus Flavius Geminus has lost his brother and now he thinks he has also lost his daughter.'

'Poor pater!' said Flavia. 'He must have been devastated.'

'He was,' said Aristo. 'He let his hair and beard grow, and we were afraid he was going to resort to unmixed wine or poppy tears, like—'

Jonathan looked up sharply.

Aristo avoided his gaze and looked at Flavia. 'When Popo and the others were kidnapped your father became obsessed with rescuing them. He went to his patron for help, and summoned his own clients. He called in every favour due to him, and recruited some powerful allies. Now he's obsessed with finding Popo.'

'Poor pater,' repeated Flavia. 'He's doing it because he thinks I'm dead.'

'I believe so,' said Aristo. 'Popo and Soso are now his closest living relatives.'

'And my parents think I'm dead,' murmured Jonathan. 'After everything that's happened . . .'

'No,' said Aristo. '*Your* parents know you're alive.'

'They do?'

Lupus grunted and opened his hands as if to say, How?

'Yes,' said Flavia, turning to Aristo. 'How do they know we're alive? And how did *you* know we were alive?'

Suddenly Lupus snapped his fingers, reached over and picked up the papyrus notice from beside Flavia. He waved it at Aristo.

'Exactly,' said their tutor grimly. 'The notices say that you were last seen in Upper Egypt. That's how we knew you must have survived the shipwreck.'

'But pater doesn't know?' said Flavia.

'No. He went in search of Popo before the notices went up.'

'Great Juno's beard,' muttered Jonathan. 'What a mess.'

'What about the other baby?' asked Nubia. 'What about Soso?'

'He's still living at Jonathan's house; the women guard him like she-tigers.'

'But the youngest wet-nurse was kidnapped with Popo?' asked Flavia.

'Yes,' said Aristo. 'I suppose they needed her to feed the baby. She's hardly more than a child herself.'

'Lydia,' said Nubia softly. 'Her name is Lydia.'

'Why doesn't someone do something about these kidnappers?' Flavia rose to her feet and twisted her hands together. 'This suppressio is so wrong. It has to stop!'

'Someone *is* doing something. Your father. He put me in charge of the household, and he took Caudex with him to Halicarnassus.'

Nubia frowned. 'I forget where is Halicarnassus.'

'In Asia,' said Aristo and Nathan together.

'I forget what is Asia, too.'

'Remember the island of Rhodes?' said Flavia. 'Where we went last year? The mainland near Rhodes is the province of Asia.'

'Is Rhodes nearby or far?' asked Nubia.

'Not far,' said Nathan. 'It's about four hundred miles north of Alexandria. Three days sailing if the winds are favourable.'

Aristo looked at Flavia. 'Your father and Caudex set sail for Halicarnassus two weeks ago. The notices went up two days later, and I set sail for Alexandria the next morning.'

'What about my parents?' asked Jonathan suddenly. 'Haven't they done anything to try to find Popo? Or me?' he added.

'No.' Aristo did not meet his gaze. 'Your father isn't well. Your mother has her hands full looking after him. She's been a tower of strength but . . .' Aristo trailed off.

Jonathan stared at the tile floor. 'Is my father still drinking poppy tears?' he asked.

'I'm afraid so. He hardly practices medicine these days. Most of his patients go to other doctors now. If it weren't for Hephzibah's riches, I don't know how your parents would survive. I'm sorry to be the one to tell you.'

'Poor doctor Mordecai,' said Flavia. 'And poor pater.'

'And poor baby Popo,' added Nubia. 'He lost father and mother, and now has been taken from his twin brother.'

Once again, Jonathan rested his head in his hands and tried to ignore the voice in his head, the voice telling him that this was all his fault.

'If we can't go home, then we have to go to Halicarnassus!' said Flavia suddenly. 'I've got to find pater and tell him I'm alive.'

'We can help him find Popo,' said Nubia.

'And the other kidnapped children,' said Flavia.

'And Lydia the wet-nurse,' said Nubia.

Lupus grunted his agreement.

'Halicarnassus,' said Nathan thoughtfully, 'That's not a bad idea. Aristo's arrival means the officials are on the alert for you again. But they probably expect you to try to get back to Italia, so it might be easier to smuggle the four of you out on a ship headed for Asia. He turned to Aristo. 'And if you decide to go with them, then I might be able to put my plan into effect immediately.'

'Of course I'll go with them,' said Aristo. 'I'm their tutor. It's my job to protect them, although I haven't had much of a chance to do that over the past few months.' He sighed. 'Also, now that Flavia knows her father is in Halicarnassus, I suspect she'll go with or without me.' He looked at Flavia. 'Am I right?'

'Absolutely,' said Flavia. 'And the sooner we go, the better.'

Early the following morning – on the Nones of August – a young Greek on his way home to Asia waited with half a dozen wheeled wooden boxes near the customs' desk at Cibotus, Alexandria's western harbour. He was in the queue to board the merchant ship *Ourania*, bound for Rhodes, Halicarnassus and Ephesus. The young man paid the export tax without question and produced a licence for his small collection of animals: a young lion, an elderly zebra, a sad-looking ostrich and two baboons.

'I'm running for office next year,' explained the youth. 'I plan to put on a small beast-fight when I return to Halicarnassus. Got this lot cheap in Naucratis.'

At his table, a sad-eyed official in a red and yellow tunic scanned a long sheet of papyrus. 'I don't have any record of you entering the city.' The official looked up at the youth.

The young Greek gave him a flashing smile. 'That's because my bride and I came through Arabia, and then up by river.' He put his arm around the veiled girl next to him and gave her shoulder a squeeze. Sad Eyes glanced briefly at the Greek's young wife. Above her veil, he could see dark hair and pale eyes. She looked to be barely more than a child, but she was heavily pregnant. Seven, perhaps eight months.

'What's wrong with this lion?' asked one of the guards, a tall Alexandrian with big, muscular thighs. He was standing on tiptoe in order to peer through the high rectangular window of the wooden cage. 'Creature's half buried in the straw,' he added. 'Only its head poking out.'

The Greek youth laughed. 'That young lion is missing its parents. The man who sold it to me said it was taken as a cub. Nestling in the straw gives it comfort. Its misery will end soon enough in the arena at Halicarnassus.'

Big Thighs looked at the young lion and the lion

stared back at him with solemn golden eyes. 'Poor little thing,' he said and moved on to the last cage. 'And these apes? Never seen apes like these before. Their eyes look almost human.' He made the sign against evil.

'Keep your distance,' warned the Greek. 'Those are Libyan baboons. They're particularly fierce. That green-eyed one nearly had my finger off the other day.'

Even as he spoke the green-eyed baboon launched himself at the small window of the wooden box, grunting angrily. The whole cage shook and Big Thighs jumped smartly back.

'Keep my distance!' he grunted. 'Right you are.' And to Sad Eyes: 'All in order.'

Sad Eyes nodded, dripped some wax on the papyrus document and pressed his official seal into it. He handed the visa back to the young Greek without looking up.

'Good voyage,' he said, waving them on. 'Next!'

SCROLL III

'Praise Juno!' breathed Flavia an hour later. 'We did it!'

She and her friends stood with Aristo at the stern of the *Ourania* and watched Alexandria recede. Flavia shaded her eyes; she thought she could see Nathan standing on the dock, a small figure in a white conical hat and sleeveless tunic. She waved her arm and the figure waved back.

Aristo sighed deeply. 'Your friend Nathan has the last of my life's savings. The visa and documents were almost as expensive as those animals. And our passage wasn't cheap either.'

'Pater will make it up to you when we get to Halicarnassus,' said Flavia. 'I know he will.' She had taken the cushion from under her long tunic and now she was pulling off the black wig. 'Oh, it feels so good to be out of that hot wig and veil!' she said.

'You can't complain,' said Jonathan. 'Nubia and Lupus and I had to put on those smelly animal skins. That was horrible.' He sniffed his own underarm. 'Ugh! I need a bath.'

Lupus nodded, grinned and imitated an ape by pulling himself along the deck by his knuckles. Then he lifted his arms and sprang up and down on bent legs, making monkey-noises.

'Lupus!' said Flavia with a shudder. 'Don't do that! It's too realistic.'

But the sailors were roaring with laughter, and when Lupus began to swing from the rigging, they all cheered. The *Ourania* was a small, elderly craft, but it was spotlessly clean and the crew seemed happy.

'At least Nathan did a good job for us,' said Flavia. 'All those papers were perfectly forged.' She batted her eyes mischievously at Aristo. 'Even our wedding certificate!' She felt Nubia stiffen beside her and quickly changed the subject: 'And I don't know how he found those animal skins.'

'Not to mention the live zebra and the ostrich,' added Jonathan, glancing back at the cages lashed to the deck.

'I'm afraid I had to sell them to Captain Artabazus,' said Aristo. He patted his coin purse and it jingled. 'It was either that or land in Halicarnassus without so much as a quadrans.'

'How much have you got?' asked Jonathan.

Aristo shrugged. 'Enough to last us a few days, if the gods are gracious.'

Flavia looked at the others. 'Speaking of the gods, we should thank them that we got out of Alexandria safely. And we should also commit our quest to them.'

'And pray we do not get shipwrecked again,' said Nubia with a shudder.

Flavia nodded and closed her eyes. 'Dear Castor and Pollux,' she prayed, 'thank you for helping us leave Alexandria. Please protect us from storms and may we not be shipwrecked again. And help us find pater, and Popo and Lydia.'

'And the other children,' added Nubia.

Lupus grunted his agreement.

Aristo closed his eyes, too. 'Help us, Lord Apollo,' he said, 'and you, too, O Neptune.'

'Dear Lord,' prayed Jonathan. 'Help us save the children.' And then he said in a voice so low that Flavia almost missed it: 'And help me atone for my sins.'

In his vision he sees Rome burn. On a citadel, the temple of Jupiter explodes and a cascade of fire roars up into the night sky. The cult statue groans in the heat, and cracks appear. The colossal head sways, topples, falls and rolls. It knocks down burning columns, bumps down the stairs past the altar, and finally comes to rest on one side, looking out over Rome with terrible blank eyes. Now the wind catches the flames from the temple and rolls them like waves, washing the city with fire. Men, women and children cry out in terror. The horses in their stables, the dogs in their kennels, the pigeons in their dovecote: all long to escape. Twenty thousand souls perish that night, among them a burning man who steps over the cliff and falls onto the traitors' rocks below.

They reached the island of Rhodes on the evening of the third day. The *Ourania* was due to offload and onload cargo, and would not set sail until the following afternoon.

The next morning, they breakfasted in Rhodes Town, under the flapping awning of a tavern overlooking the town square. The sound of the wind chimes brought back all the memories of the previous year to Lupus.

The other three had never had a chance to see the fallen Colossus up close, and Aristo had never been to Rhodes, so after a morning at the baths, Lupus led them up the hill to the sanctuary of Apollo, where the massive bronze head lay on the ground.

On his previous visit, the rhododendron bushes had been in bloom. Now, in the pounding midday heat, the grasses on the hillside were dried and golden, and the rhododendrons dusty.

While Aristo and his friends examined the head up close, Lupus stood at a distance and watched them. He remembered how the little slave-dealer called Magnus and his big mute henchman Ursus had pursued him around the pieces of the fallen statue, and how they had tried to kill him. Lupus had trapped the little one and knocked the big one unconscious, but later they had both escaped. Lupus wondered if they had joined Biggest Buyer in Halicarnassus.

He turned and looked down the hill towards the votive tree, its thousand copper plaques blazing in the afternoon sunshine like a golden fleece. He had dedicated a plaque there, asking for healing for his tongue, and now he briefly considered going down to see if his prayer was still there. But how could his tongue be healed? The slave-dealer had cut it off in order to prevent him from naming a murderer. How could something that no longer existed be restored? Lupus angrily kicked at the dust and when he turned back, the colossal head swam in a blur of tears.

As the *Ourania* set sail for Halicarnassus with the afternoon breeze, Flavia stood in the bows, lost in memories of her own. She was thinking of Gaius Valerius Flaccus, the handsome young patrician who had helped them break the illegal slave trade in Rhodes the previous year. He had gone on to Asia to try to uncover the mastermind behind the operation, the man they had nicknamed Biggest Buyer. Later – back in Ostia – Flaccus had nobly defended a slave-girl charged with murder.

When he had proposed marriage to Flavia in February she had turned him down, not because she didn't like him, but because she had impulsively made a vow never to marry. Now she felt a flush of shame at the memory of their last encounter. She could hear herself telling him she had renounced men and that she was going to be a virgin huntress like the goddess Diana. A virgin huntress! How childish he must have thought her.

She lifted her face to let the sea breeze cool her hot cheeks, remembering his response: *Your arrow has pierced my heart*. He had plucked one of the arrows from her quiver and broken it and kept the pointed half for himself.

'Oh Floppy!' she whispered. 'Do you still have my arrow? Or have you found someone else?' Beneath her feet, the *Ourania*'s deck gently rose, paused and dipped, rose, paused and dipped, as if expressing the slow heart-beat of the sea.

Out of the corner of her eye, Flavia saw a movement. Nubia and Aristo were standing a few paces away, speaking quietly together. Nubia's short black hair was plaited and oiled, and around her shoulders she wore a fringed silk palla in orange, dark blue and gold. Aristo was smiling and Nubia's golden eyes shone; she looked beautiful. Flavia felt a pang of jealousy, then instantly felt guilty for being jealous.

Presently, Aristo went back towards the stern and Nubia came to join her.

'What were you and Aristo talking about?' asked Flavia. 'He seemed happy.'

Nubia pulled her palla around her shoulders. 'He asked me to play music with him tonight. He says he wants to play joyful music since he discovers the four of us are still alive. He says for him the world has colour again.'

Flavia turned and caught her friend's hands. 'Nubia, don't let this opportunity slip away. Tell him how you feel.'

Nubia lowered her eyes. 'I am afraid,' she said. 'It is so wonderful that we can play music together again. I do not want to lose that.'

'I know you're afraid to tell him you love him, but . . . Listen, Nubia: I turned down Floppy when he proposed and—' Flavia was surprised by the strength of emotion that suddenly overwhelmed her. Her eyes brimmed and her throat felt tight.

'And you wish you had not?' asked Nubia gently.

Flavia nodded and began to cry. 'Oh, Nubia,' she sobbed. 'I think I love him. But what if he thinks I'm dead? What if he's married someone else?'

The two girls embraced and held each other tightly as the ship rose and fell beneath them.

After a while Flavia pulled a handkerchief from her belt pouch and blew her nose. She stared towards the blue horizon and sighed. Her tears had brought some relief.

Nubia also stared ahead. 'Chrysis said something to me when we were travelling together along the bank of the Nile,' she said.

'What?'

'The same thing you said. That I should be brave and tell Aristo how I feel.'

'And you should!' said Flavia, gripping her friend's hands. 'You are so beautiful and gentle. Any man would be lucky to have you.'

Nubia's golden eyes were brimming now, too. 'That is just what Chrysis said. But I must wait for the right moment.'

Flavia sighed and looked at her friend with deep affection. 'All right,' she said. 'But none of us know what the gods have in store for us. Don't make the same mistake I did. Nubia, don't wait too long.'

SCROLL IV

They passed Lupus's home island Symi later that afternoon and the beautiful marble port of Cnidos in the golden evening. That night they anchored beneath a full moon in a cove of the volcanic island of Nisyrus. The faint eggy smell of sulphur mingled with the fresh green scent of pine trees on the shore.

The next morning they woke to the sound of a joyful dawn chorus of a thousand tiny birds in the conifers. The birds were still singing when they weighed anchor, and they took this for a good omen.

An hour before noon, the merchant ship *Ourania* sailed into a sunny port surrounded by hills. The slopes of the hills reminded Jonathan of the seating in a theatre and the harbour was like its circular blue orchestra.

'Is this Halicarnassus?' asked Nubia, pulling her fluttering shawl tighter around her shoulders. 'Halicarnassus in Asia?'

'According to Captain Artabazus it is,' said Jonathan.

'Halicarnassus!' proclaimed Flavia. 'Home of Herodotus the father of history and site of the tomb of Mausolus, also known as the Mausoleum, one of the Seven Sights of the world. Correct?' She looked over her shoulder at Aristo who had come to stand behind them.

'Yes, Flavia.' He gave Jonathan a wink. 'You're correct. As usual.'

Lupus grunted and pointed towards a monument rising above the roofs of the town: a gleaming white pyramid raised high on columns and topped with a painted sculpture of two figures in a chariot.

'Lupus is right,' said Jonathan. 'That must be the Mausoleum.'

'But do you know what the first tomb of Mausolus was?' said Flavia. 'It was his wife, Artemisia!'

Nubia turned her golden eyes on Flavia. 'How?'

'She loved him so much that after he died she drank his ashes mixed in wine, so that she could be his tomb. His living tomb.'

Lupus pretended to gag and Flavia nodded sagely. 'She died two years later, of grief.'

'Or of drinking a dead man's ashes,' muttered Jonathan under his breath.

Flavia ignored him. 'But before Artemisia died, she commissioned the most magnificent tomb in the world, and that's it. She's buried there, too, with her beloved Mausolus. And now it's considered one of the Seven Sights of—'

'You just said that,' snapped Jonathan, 'you don't have to tell us a thousand times.' The injured look on Flavia's face immediately made him regret his words, but before he could find the energy to apologise, Captain Artabazus came up beside them and rested his hairy forearms on the polished rail.

'Where are all the townspeople?' He glared around as the *Ourania* approached one of the berths. 'The whole place is deserted. Where's the harbour master? Where are all the other sailors and captains? It looks as if a plague has struck.'

Jonathan saw the others make the sign against evil.

Captain Artabazus turned and addressed the crew in his seaman's bellow: 'Who's willing to go down and find out what's happening? Has anybody here had plague?'

'I'll go,' said Jonathan, raising his hand.

Lupus grunted in alarm and Nubia whispered: 'Jonathan! You have not had the plague.'

Jonathan shrugged. 'I've had the fever,' he said.

'But that's different,' said Flavia. 'Plague is much worse than fever.'

'They're right,' said Aristo. 'If there's a plague then it would be suicide to disembark.'

'I said I'll go!' snapped Jonathan. And under his breath he added: 'If I die, I die.'

Half an hour later, Nubia followed Flavia carefully down the gangplank. She took Aristo's outstretched hand and jumped lightly onto the wooden dock.

'Where did you say everyone had gone?' Flavia was asking Jonathan. 'It sounded like you said the whole town's at the theatre!'

Nubia looked around. She was in the great port of Halicarnassus, in Asia, but it looked very much like the port of Ostia out of season. There were only a few fishermen here, mending their nets, and some sailors playing knucklebones in the shade of a warehouse.

'That's right,' said Jonathan. 'Practically everybody is at the theatre. No point looking for your father, yet. Those fishermen told me all the offices are closed. We're in luck,' he added under his breath. 'The customs' stall is unmanned.'

'Why is everyone at the theatre?' said Aristo. 'Today's not a festival, is it?'

Lupus did a back flip and then took a bow like a pantomime dancer.

'It's not a festival and there's no pantomime,' said Jonathan, and nodded towards the fishermen. 'They said a travelling magician is speaking there.'

'Let's go, then,' said Flavia. 'Maybe we'll find pater there. But first, we need to give thanks for arriving safely.'

'And we need to do it without being detected,' murmured Aristo. He looked up at the sound of a whistle and saw that one of the sailors on the *Ourania* was about to toss down his leather travelling satchel. 'Can you keep our things on board,' he called out, 'until I send someone to get them? I'm not sure where we're staying yet.'

'No problem,' said the sailor. 'We're here until tomorrow morning.'

'Wait,' cried Flavia as the sailor turned back. 'Do you know Halicarnassus?'

'A little.'

'Is there a temple or shrine to Neptune here? So we can make a thanks offering?'

The sailor pointed a muscular forearm. 'Just beyond those shops there,' he said. 'Little temple to Poseidon. That's what they call him in this part of the world.'

Nubia followed the others across the wooden docks and past warehouses towards some shops on the north side of the harbour. The shops were shuttered up but one stall near the temple sold votive honey cakes and live doves.

Aristo paid for a white dove and took it over to the altar at the foot of the temple steps. There was no sign of the priest, so Aristo sacrificed the dove himself. Nubia averted her eyes as Aristo wrung the dove's neck and dripped its bright red blood on the altar. She knew it was right to give thanks for their safe voyage, but she hated the way it was done.

As they started towards the theatre, Nubia glanced up at Aristo. 'Why did you sacrifice the dove?' she asked softly.

He sighed. 'I vowed to give Poseidon a thanks offering if he brought us safely here. A dove was all I can afford.'

'But why a living creature?'

'They're worth more than cakes or fruit. Because of the blood.'

'But why blood?'

Jonathan answered: 'Because the life is in the blood.'

'Oh,' said Nubia. She still did not understand.

On the other side of Aristo, Lupus grunted and pointed at a man pushing a cart in the middle of the street a short distance ahead of them. The cart was full of sesame-seed bread rolls, each about the size of a bracelet.

'You're hungry?' Aristo said to Lupus. 'And you want a sesame ring?'

Lupus nodded and Jonathan said, 'I'm starving.' He was wheezing a little because of the steepness of the hill they were climbing.

'Me, too,' said Flavia.

Nubia still felt slightly off-balance, as she always did after a few days at sea, and she was queasy from watching the sacrifice. Even so, her stomach growled.

Aristo grinned. 'Here, Lupus!' He flipped Lupus a drachma. 'Catch him up.'

Lupus ran up the hill to catch the bread-seller. He was

taking his bread rings and change when they reached him. The great Mausoleum loomed above them a few streets to their right. Nubia was glad to stop climbing for a moment and gaze up at it.

'Do you know what's happening up at the theatre?' Aristo asked the bread-ring-seller when he had caught his breath.

'Not sure,' said the man cheerfully. 'Prophet, philosopher, magician, healer. These days Asia is crawling with them; we get one coming through every month or so. But I never go to see them. If I went in with the others, I'd never earn a mite, would I?' He gave them a gap-toothed grin and carried on pushing his cart up towards the theatre.

Nubia took a tentative bite of her sesame-seed ring: it was still warm and it was delicious, but after she swallowed it sat like a pebble in her stomach. She put the rest in her belt-pouch for later.

Lupus was clowning for them, pretending to wear his bread-ring as a bracelet.

Jonathan glared at him. 'Stop playing the fool,' he wheezed. 'If you aren't going to eat that, give it to me.'

Lupus glared at him and defiantly took a bite, but he didn't chew carefully enough and had a coughing fit as it went down the wrong way.

Jonathan gave him a violent smack between the shoulder blades. This action successfully dislodged the piece of bread, but the force of the blow was so great that it brought tears to Lupus's eyes.

'Jonathan,' gasped Nubia. 'You hit Lupus too hard.'

'Yes, Jonathan,' said Flavia. 'What's got into you these past days? You've always been a pessimist but you've never been mean before.'

'Jonathan,' said Nubia. 'Is something wrong?'

Jonathan silenced her with a glare and they followed Aristo up the hill in silence. The houses here were all whitewashed and some had colourful flower boxes on the upper floor balconies.

A moment later, they emerged into an open space and Nubia's eyes grew wide.

A crowd of excited citizens seethed around the theatre entrance like bees on a honeycomb. Standing a little apart from the crowd was a group of emaciated figures in rags; they stared longingly at the theatre.

'Careful,' said Aristo, panting a little. 'They're lepers. If you touch them, you'll catch their disease.' He mopped his sweating forehead and neck with a handkerchief.

The lepers stood in silence but many others in the crowd were crying and pleading to be let in.

'Help me go in!' Nubia heard a woman cry. 'I need him to heal me!'

'My daughter's ill,' sobbed a man, carrying a little girl in his arms. 'Let us through. Please!'

'He's just a trickster!' grumbled an old man at the edge of the crowd.

'Sour grapes,' cackled another. 'You're just saying that because they won't let you in. I've heard he makes the deaf hear and the dumb talk.'

Nubia glanced at Lupus to see if he had heard the man's words. The magician in the theatre could make the dumb talk.

Lupus stood staring towards the theatre, his arms slack and his bread-ring in one hand, forgotten. She saw the gleam of hope in his eyes and her heart melted for him.

SCROLL V

Lupus saw men and women tugging at people's garments, pleading to be let through. The magician was in the theatre, apparently making the blind see, the deaf hear and the dumb talk. Lupus handed his half-eaten sesame-ring to Nubia and dropped onto his hands and knees. He tried to crawl through the forest of legs, but the crowd was too dense. He was jostled, shoved and kicked. When a fat man nearly brought his hobnailed boot down onto Lupus's hand, he retreated and limped back to where his friends were waiting. He was no longer a scrawny beggar boy living wild in Ostia's graveyard. Two years of eating proper meals and sleeping in a soft warm bed had added a foot to his height and given him bulk.

Lupus shaded his eyes against the bright noonday sun and glanced around. There had to be another way to get in there. Or at least to see what was happening.

The theatre was at the outskirts of town, on a hillside. On the western side of the theatre stood three tall poplar trees. Lupus tugged Aristo's tunic, pointed to the nearest poplar and imitated climbing.

'You want a leg up?' asked Aristo.

Lupus grunted yes.

'That's a good idea,' said Flavia. 'I don't think there's

any other way to see what's happening in there.'

'All right,' said Aristo with a sigh. 'But don't fall out.'

The five of them were climbing the hill towards the poplar trees when they heard a bellow like that of a wounded ox. Lupus and the others turned back to see a huge man forcing his way out of the theatre and through the seething mass. The man was so tall that his head and shoulders rose above the crowd as he pushed towards them.

Suddenly Lupus grunted in disbelief as he recognised the giant. It was Ursus, the big mute bodyguard who had pursued him around the fallen Colossus of Rhodes the year before.

Ursus's mouth was open in a horrifying grin and his eyes were fixed in a maniacal stare. He was bellowing at the top of his lungs and now that he was free of the screaming crowd, he was running straight towards them.

Nubia felt Aristo grasp her shoulder. 'Quickly!' he cried. 'Behind this altar!'

He pulled her back with one hand and Flavia with the other and they crouched behind the altar with Jonathan and Lupus.

Nubia could hear the giant's roar getting closer and closer. She leaned back against Aristo's shoulder and closed her eyes, feeling a strange mixture of euphoria and fear: euphoria from being so close to Aristo and fear of the yelling man.

The bellowing giant was almost upon them. Nubia could feel Aristo's heart pounding against her back. The smell of blood and charred flesh from the remains of the lamb on the altar made her feel dizzy and she thought she might swoon in his arms again.

But now the giant had passed by, and already the sound of his cry was getting fainter as he disappeared around a corner.

'What was that?' wheezed Jonathan, standing up and shading his eyes to gaze in the direction the giant had gone.

'*Who* was that?' said Flavia.

Nubia gratefully clung to Aristo's arm as he helped her rise to her feet; she still felt dizzy.

Lupus dipped his finger in a trickle of blood dripping down the side of the altar and wrote on the white marble: URSUS. BODYGUARD OF MAGNUS.

'The one who tried to kill you in Rhodes?' asked Jonathan.

Lupus nodded and wiped his finger on his tunic. Then he pointed urgently in the direction the giant had gone and beckoned them on.

'What?' cried Aristo. 'You want us to follow him?'

Lupus nodded vigorously and Flavia cried, 'Yes! Ursus worked for Magnus, and Magnus worked for Biggest Buyer. If we follow him, he might lead us to the kidnapped children. And maybe to Popo.'

Aristo hesitated.

'The gods have answered our prayers,' said Flavia. 'They led us right to him.'

Nubia caught Aristo's hand and gazed up into his beautiful face. 'This is our chance,' she pleaded. 'Our chance to help the children.'

'All right then,' he said, giving her hand a squeeze in return. 'Come on.'

★

The oven-hot streets of Halicarnassus were still deserted, and it was easy to track Ursus through the western part of the city to the Myndus Gate. Unveiled women were still leaning out of upstairs windows and children stared open-mouthed in the direction he had gone. As they passed through the shaded arch of the town gate, Flavia caught sight of a man in a straw sunhat sitting in the shade of an olive tree, between two tombs. His two-wheeled mule cart stood nearby.

'Have you just seen a giant running by?' she asked, speaking Latin in her excitement.

The man looked up from carving a piece of cheese and stared at her blankly.

'Have you just seen a giant running past?' asked Aristo in Greek.

The man nodded and stood up and pointed west. He wore a sleeveless tunic and his skin was very brown; he was obviously a farmer. 'Just a few moments ago,' he said, also in Greek. 'He was heading down the Myndus road.'

'Is that your chariot?' asked Flavia in Greek. She couldn't remember the Greek word for cart.

'Yes,' he grinned. 'And that's my brave steed. We've just been to the market to unload some heroic watermelons.'

'I'll pay you two drachmas if you take us in your cart and help us catch him,' said Aristo.

'I'll do it for four,' said the farmer.

'Done,' said Aristo. He gave the man a silver tetradrachm. Flavia knew it was one of his last coins, and as they all climbed up into the cart, she offered a silent prayer to Castor and Pollux for more funds.

The farmer flicked his mule into a trot. It was only a

two-wheeled vegetable cart and the four friends and their tutor had to stand crowded together and clutching at the wooden sides.

As they left Halicarnassus behind them, Flavia looked around. The sun blazed in a pure blue sky and the air shimmered with heat. The cart rode almost silently on the dusty verge of the road, and she could hear the throb of cicadas that filled the silvery-green olive trees beyond the tombs lining the road out of town. Apart from the strong scent of thyme, and the Greek inscriptions on the tombs, they might have been on one of the roads outside Rome. She felt a pang of homesickness. Would she ever get back home to her beloved Ostia?

Suddenly Lupus grunted and pointed.

'Yes!' cried Flavia, shading her eyes with her hand. 'There he is! I can see him running up ahead!'

'Great Juno's beard,' muttered Jonathan. 'He's been running for half an hour without stopping. Is he mad?'

'I thought he was going to attack us back there by the theatre,' said Flavia. 'Didn't you, Lupus?'

Without taking his eyes from the distant figure trembling in the heat haze on the road ahead, Lupus nodded.

'I'm sure Ursus saw us,' said Jonathan. 'He was looking right at us.'

Lupus nodded again.

'So why did he run past us?' mused Flavia.

Lupus shrugged.

'Maybe he wasn't after us,' said Flavia. 'Maybe he was chasing someone else.'

'Maybe he wasn't after anyone,' said Jonathan. 'He looked berserk.'

'He looked terrified,' said Flavia.

Nubia was frowning thoughtfully. 'No,' she said. 'Not terrified. Happy.'

The three of them turned to stare at Nubia.

'Happy?' said Flavia in disbelief. 'You thought he looked *happy*?'

'Crazy happy?' ventured Nubia.

'I don't think so,' snorted Flavia, and she tapped Aristo's shoulder. 'Ask the driver to slow down a little. We don't want Ursus to see us following him.'

Aristo nodded and repeated Flavia's request in Greek. The farmer pulled slightly on the reins and the mule slowed.

'Behold!' said Nubia presently. 'The giant goes off from the road.'

'Yes,' said Flavia. 'He's cutting across the field. Look. There's a villa over there. See the red tiles of the roof just peeking above the olive trees on the hillside?'

'I think you're right,' said Aristo. 'That double row of cypress trees further ahead marks a road leading up to an estate. That must be where he's going.'

Lupus tugged the back of Aristo's tunic. He pointed after Ursus, who had disappeared into an olive grove. Then Lupus pointed at himself.

'You want to follow him on foot?'

Lupus nodded and as the cart slowed he leapt off and started across the scrubby field after Ursus.

'Lupus!' called Aristo. 'We'll meet you at the turning! At the place where the tree-lined drive begins! In an hour!'

Without turning around, Lupus gave them a thumbs-up.

'Be careful!' cried Aristo, and shook his head. 'I don't like it,' he muttered, as the farmer flicked his mule into motion again. 'I don't like him going after that giant by himself.'

'Lupus will be all right,' said Flavia, then added under her breath. 'Please Juno, may Lupus be all right.' She looked at Aristo. 'What's our plan?'

But before Aristo could answer, Nubia pointed.

'Behold!' she said. 'I see a carruca waiting in shadow of trees!'

'Strange,' muttered Jonathan. 'They look like soldiers.'

Flavia squinted and shaded her eyes. 'The sun's so bright,' she murmured.

'Here,' said the farmer in Greek. 'Have my hat.' He removed his straw sunhat and put it on Flavia's head.

'Thank you,' said Flavia. 'That does help.'

They were closer now and she could see a carruca standing in the shadows of the cypress trees. Half a dozen soldiers were coming down off it, directed by a short man with a patrician toga and thinning hair. Even from a distance he looked familiar. Then the man in the toga turned; and she instantly recognised his pale eyes.

'Great Juno's peacock!' she gasped. 'It's Ostia's magistrate, Marcus Artorius Bato.'

SCROLL VI

'Flavia Gemina and company!' Bato raised his eyebrows. 'Why am I not surprised to find you here, alive and well despite all reports to the contrary?'

The farmer had let them off at the turning of the tree-lined avenue, and now they stood before Bato and his men.

'We're here to find a criminal mastermind,' said Flavia, 'and to rescue some kidnapped children.' She spoke as coldly as possible. Half a year ago Bato had slandered them all in court. He had called Flavia a big-nosed busybody.

'And what?' said Bato drily. 'You were going to charge in with your little army here?' He glanced at her hat. 'Disguised as a farmer? I've got an imperial mandate. What have you got?' Bato mopped his high forehead with a handkerchief. He looked hot and irritated.

Flavia opened her mouth and then closed it again.

'You've got an imperial mandate?' said Aristo.

Bato sighed, nodded and pulled a slender parchment scroll from his belt. 'This allows me to question all the slaves, and to take away any we suspect might be freeborn. If we find even one who has been illegally imprisoned, or the least evidence of suppressio, then we can arrest the owner of this villa.'

'Euge!' breathed Nubia, clapping her hands. 'We can set free the captured children.'

'Not so fast,' said Flavia, holding up a hand to stop Nubia and narrowing her eyes at Bato. 'You can't arrest someone unless a private citizen is willing to take them to court. I learned that last year.'

Bato sighed deeply. 'Your father and I intend to take him to court,' he said, 'and we hope to return the captured children to their families.'

'Pater?' Flavia's anger at Bato instantly evaporated. 'You're here with pater?'

Bato nodded. 'He helped fund this expedition.'

'Where is he?' Flavia looked eagerly around.

'He went to Rhodes to investigate the report of a baby who might be his little nephew.'

'Pater went to Rhodes? When?'

'Two days ago.'

'Oh, no!' cried Flavia. 'We thought he was in Halicarnassus. That's why we came here.' She felt the tears well up. Her hopes of seeing him had been so high, but now she wondered if she would ever see him again.

'Do you think Popo is in Rhodes?' asked Jonathan.

Bato shook his head. 'It was just a rumour of a report. It's more likely that your little nephew is with the other kidnapped children in that villa.' He nodded down the tree-lined lane towards the villa. 'It belongs to a man called Lucius Mindius Faustus. We think Mindius is behind the kidnappings of the past few years.'

'Mindius?' said Flavia. 'Don't you mean Magnus?'

'Magnus was working for Mindius,' said Bato. 'Mindius is the mastermind behind most of the illegal slave trade in the Roman Empire.'

'He's Biggest Buyer?' breathed Flavia.

'We're almost certain of it. We were going to raid him next week, but when I heard a popular travelling prophet was going to be in town today, I decided to do it today.'

'Can we do something to help?' asked Jonathan.

Bato shook his head. 'Our plan worked. Look. The gates are lying wide open. All his guards must have gone to the theatre.'

'Like Ursus!' cried Flavia. 'He was at the theatre.'

Bato gave her a sharp look. 'Ursus?' he said. 'The big mute giant?'

'Yes,' said Jonathan. 'We saw him running this way a short time ago, bellowing like a bull.'

Bato's face grew pale. 'Did he see you?'

The friends glanced at each other.

'Yes,' said Flavia in a small voice.

'We've been planning this raid for days,' said Bato from between clenched teeth. 'Mindius and Ursus know your faces and they know mine. I've been careful not to let either of them see me.' He glared at Flavia. 'It took a lot of time and money to obtain this warrant. If Ursus saw you and suspected a raid, if the abducted children have been taken somewhere else, and if we lose our chance to rescue them, then it will be your fault.'

'Oh, no,' said Flavia weakly.

'Oh, yes, Flavia Gemina. Oh, yes.'

The large, cool atrium of the opulent villa was deserted. It was so quiet that Nubia could hear a fountain splashing somewhere deeper inside and the cicadas creaking in the olive groves outside. There was a faint smell of incense and the strong smell of lavender.

Bato led his clinking soldiers quickly around the shallow impluvium and into an inner garden. As Nubia and the others hurried after him, she offered up a silent prayer: Please let the children be here!

The garden's centrepiece was a splashing fountain surrounded by beds of fragrant herbs planted in diamonds and circle patterns. A columned and shaded walkway surrounded the garden, with a dozen rooms giving onto it.

As Bato and his men began to search these rooms, Nubia thought she saw a small movement behind a lavender bush near the fountain. She stepped into the blazing light and heat of the garden, then crouched down and addressed the shrub.

'Come out,' she whispered in Greek. 'We will not hurt you.'

The lavender bush did not reply.

'We will not hurt you.' This time she said it in Latin, and the bush stirred slightly.

'The soldiers will not hurt you either,' Nubia continued in Latin. 'They just want to take you home.'

'Home to mummy and daddy?' the bush replied in muffled Latin.

Nubia glanced over at Aristo and Flavia, who had stopped to watch her from the shaded peristyle.

'Yes,' she said in Latin. 'Home to mummy and daddy.'

The branches of the shrub parted and a little boy of about four years old appeared, sucking his thumb. He was thin and grubby and pale.

'What is your name?' asked Nubia gently.

'Gaius.' The boy took his thumb out of his mouth. 'Gaius Cartilius Poplicola.'

'Great Juno's peacock!' Flavia ran forward to join Nubia. 'He's from Ostia.'

'From one its most illustrious families,' added Aristo,

stepping into the bright sunlight. 'He must be one of the children kidnapped last month!'

'Have you found someone?' called Bato, appearing in the shadowy doorway of a bedroom. When they nodded, he said: 'Ask him where the others are.'

'I'm hungry,' said Gaius.

Nubia opened her belt pouch and pulled out the sesame-seed bread ring that Aristo had bought that morning. She broke it in half and handed him a piece. The little boy devoured it greedily, then held out his hand for the other half.

'What happened?' said Nubia. 'Where is everybody?'

'We heard Big Bear yelling,' said Gaius. 'He sounded angry, so I hid.'

'Ursus?' said Flavia. 'Do you mean Ursus? About half an hour ago?'

The little boy nodded, and Nubia gave him the other half of the sesame ring.

'Are there any other children here?' asked Nubia softly. 'Is anyone else hiding?'

'My friends are making carpets,' said Gaius, his mouth full. 'But someone else is hiding. One of the bad men.'

'One of the men who enslaved you?' cried Flavia.

'Yes,' said Gaius. He swallowed the last of the bread-ring and pointed a grubby finger. 'When he heard you coming he hid in that room over there.'

Nubia glanced at Aristo. He nodded bravely back at her, so she whispered to Gaius. 'Will you show me?' She felt his hot little hand grip her fingers and let him lead her around the fountain, beneath the colonnade and into the cool tablinum. There was a desk here, and scroll niches on the wall and in one corner a small cupboard. Nubia knew it was the kind of cupboard in which

Romans stored their family death masks. Gaius stopped before this cupboard and pointed with his free hand.

'What is it?' asked Jonathan, who had just come in with two soldiers. 'What's happening?'

'Someone's hiding in there,' said Flavia. 'We think.'

'How can a man be hiding in there?' said Jonathan, frowning at the cupboard.

Nubia nodded. 'It is too small.'

Aristo stepped towards the cupboard, took a deep breath, then reached out to pull the little ivory knob at the top of the biggest door. At first the door seemed stuck, then it flew open and both Flavia and Nubia jumped back with a squeal.

There were no death masks in the cupboard. It contained a crouching dwarf.

'Behold!' cried Nubia. 'It is Magnus the dwarf!'

SCROLL VII

'Bato, come quickly!' cried Flavia, as Aristo grasped the little man's arm and pulled him out of the cupboard. 'It's Magnus! The slave-dealer from Rhodes.'

'So I see.' Bato sneered down at the dwarf. 'The little slave-trader who used to ride on the shoulders of his giant bodyguard,' he said. 'We meet again.'

Magnus lifted his head. His handsome face was contorted with hatred.

'I could smell you a mile off,' he sneered. 'You politicians all stink.'

'If you could smell me a mile off,' said Bato, with a sneer of his own, 'then why did you linger?' Bato beckoned two of his soldiers. 'Put the manacles on this one. I don't want him to get away again. Tell me, little man, where is your master?'

Magnus snarled as one of the soldiers pulled his hands behind his back and fastened stiff leather manacles on his wrists. 'Mindius is not my master!' he said. 'He's my patron. We're partners.'

'Partners in the business of suppressio,' said Bato. 'You disgust me. How can you enslave freeborn children like this?' He gestured towards little Gaius, who was hiding behind Nubia.

'Slaves keep the empire running smoothly,' said

Magnus. 'We haven't had any wars recently, so supplies of captives are running low. Mindius and I are just filling a gap in the market. We're doing you all a service.'

'But it's illegal to enslave freeborn children,' cried Flavia. 'And it's wrong.'

Magnus glared up at her. 'Well, Miss Straw Hat, why don't you tell that to their parents? These children may be freeborn, but half of them were sold to us by their parents in order to pay their debts. We give them shelter, food and a useful occupation.'

'Oh yes,' said Bato, his voice heavy with sarcasm. 'You're doing a great public service.'

Flavia folded her arms. 'Where is my cousin Popo?' she said coldly.

'Yes,' said Jonathan. 'Why did you kidnap my sister's baby? He never did anything to hurt you!'

The dwarf's handsome face went blank for a moment, then understanding dawned and he sneered. 'Why do you think we took him?' he said.

'Was it to get revenge on us for thwarting you last year?' asked Flavia.

'Why would I want revenge on you?' he said, his voice heavy with sarcasm. 'Do you think it might be because you destroyed my business, ran me out of my home and humiliated me in front of the entire population of Rhodes?'

Flavia and Jonathan exchanged a helpless glance.

'Where are the other children?' asked Nubia.

'Yes,' said Bato. 'Show us where the other children are.'

Magnus's smile vanished. 'Find them yourself.'

'I'll show you,' piped a child's voice. Little Gaius

emerged from behind Nubia and held out his hand to Bato.

'Thank you,' said Bato to the little boy, and to his soldiers: 'Take the dwarf back to Halicarnassus, lock him up in the basilica cells.'

Flavia watched the two soldiers escort Magnus out of the tablinum and along the colonnade towards the main entrance, then she turned to follow the others.

Clutching Bato's hand, little Gaius led them through the fountain courtyard and out through the back of the villa into the pounding heat and brilliant light of the afternoon. Behind the vegetable garden and the stables was a wooden shed. Flavia followed the others inside.

'By Hercules!' cried Bato, and she heard Nubia gasp.

It was hot in here, and dim. She recoiled at the stench of urine mixed with the unpleasant garlic-seaweed smell of purple dye. As her eyes adjusted to the darkness, she saw twenty or twenty-five children, sitting before looms and weaving grimly.

'Great Juno's peacock!' she murmured.

The children's hair was lank, their eyes swollen and their skin chalky white. Some of them were coughing weakly.

Bato pulled out his handkerchief and held it to his nose. 'Poor creatures,' he said. 'Chained to the looms. It looks as if they've been beaten as well.' He stepped forward to examine two little girls, one dark and one fair.

But as he approached, the girls cringed and whimpered, so Bato stopped and turned to Flavia.

'Will you reassure them? Just until we find the key to unlock them.'

Flavia knelt in the straw beside the oldest girl.

'My name's Flavia Gemina,' she said in Latin. 'That's my friend Nubia, and Jonathan's the one with dark curly hair, and that's our tutor Aristo. The man in the toga, holding hands with Gaius, he's Bato. We've come to set you free! What's your name?'

The girl was eight or nine, with sallow skin and lank dark hair. She did not reply but the younger girl beside her whispered: 'Salome doesn't speak Latin.'

'But you do?'

The little girl nodded.

'What's your name?'

The little girl looked at Flavia with swollen eyes. Her skin was bitten by fleas and her fingertips were raw. 'Are you a boy or a girl?' whispered the girl.

Flavia smiled and took off her straw sunhat and shook out her shoulder-length hair. 'I'm a girl. My name is Flavia. Do they make you weave carpets all day?'

The little girl nodded, then whispered, 'My name is like yours.'

'What is it?' Flavia made herself smile.

'Flavilla. My name is Flavilla.'

'Flavilla?' said Flavia gently, 'What happened to your fingers? Did you burn them?'

Flavilla looked at Flavia with her red-rimmed eyes. 'If we cut our fingers they burn them, so we don't bleed on the wool,' she whispered.

'Oh, you poor thing,' whispered Flavia, and she felt tears prick her eyes.

Flavilla's eyes were also filling with tears. 'And they beat us if we don't do enough. And they don't let us use the latrine.' Her lower lip began to quiver.

'Don't cry, Flavilla,' said Flavia. 'You don't have to weave any more and as soon as we find the key, we'll let you go free.' And to Salome, Flavia said in Greek. 'You're going to be free.'

'That's right,' said Bato in Greek. 'We're here to end this.'

'Flavia,' said Jonathan. 'Ask her about Popo.'

Flavia nodded. 'Flavilla,' she said. 'Is there a baby here? A little baby boy about seven or eight months old?'

Flavilla frowned. 'I don't think so,' she said. 'I think a baby is too little to weave.'

'Or a girl called Lydia?' said Nubia. 'With blue eyes and light brown hair like yours?

Flavilla shook her head.

'I saw a baby,' said little Gaius, who was still holding Bato's hand. 'Fusty took him with him when he ran away.'

'Fusty?'

'I think he means Mindius,' said Bato. 'Lucius Mindius Faustus is his full name.'

Nubia crouched down in front of Gaius. 'Did Fusty run away?'

Gaius nodded. 'He and Big Bear and the baby and the baby's mummy all rode away. On horsies.'

'And they took the baby with them?' said Flavia.

Little Gaius nodded, his brown eyes wide.

'When?' said Bato, also squatting down before the little boy. 'When did he leave?'

'A long time ago,' said Gaius. For a moment his forehead wrinkled in a frown of concentration, then he said. 'Twice as long as it takes me to count to a hundred.'

Lupus emerged from the sun-dappled olive groves into the pounding heat of early afternoon. It was the hottest time of the day and the throb of the cicadas was almost deafening. He had lost Ursus in the olive grove but at least he had found the red-roofed villa.

The rhythmic roar of the cicadas was so great that he didn't hear the thunder of horses' hooves until they were almost upon him.

With a grunt of alarm, he threw himself out of the way just as the lead horse galloped past. It was a massive black gelding with a white blaze, and its rider was Ursus, the giant. For a moment his eyes locked with Lupus's. By the time Lupus tore his gaze away to look at the others, they were almost past and the dust was rising up behind them, obscuring them from sight. But he had managed to catch a glimpse. The second rider had been a man: dark eyes in a yellowish face, between forty and fifty years old. The third rider had been a veiled woman with a bundle strapped to her front.

Lupus stood and dusted himself off. Then he froze. He just realised what he had seen. It had not been a bundle lashed to the woman's body.

It had been a baby.

Twenty-five children aged between four and thirteen were gathered in the cool atrium of the villa outside Halicarnassus. Some looked around in wonder; they had never been in this part of the villa before. Others were fascinated by the soldiers' armour. Most were coughing, all were thin. Their eyes were red-rimmed and their fingertips bloody or calloused. Little Gaius stood sucking a corner of Bato's toga as the magistrate tallied the number of children on his wax tablet.

One of Bato's soldiers had made up a batch of posca and was passing round a tray of mismatched beakers and goblets.

Suddenly Lupus hurried into the atrium, waving his wax tablet.

'Lupus!' cried Flavia. 'You just missed Magnus the dwarf! We arrested him.'

Two sweating soldiers jogged into the atrium after Lupus, the jingle of their armour echoed in the cool lofty space. 'This boy,' puffed one of the soldiers, 'saw three riders heading northeast.'

'Sextus and Decimus,' said the other, 'are in pursuit.'

'Three riders on horseback?' exclaimed Bato. He looked at Lupus. 'Was one of them a dark-haired man in his forties? Did he look like that?'

Bato gestured towards an encaustic portrait on the wall in a corner of the atrium, where most Roman houses had a lararium.

Lupus moved through the children to examine the painting. It showed a middle-aged man with dark hair and large brown eyes. Although the portrait was idealised, Lupus recognised the man. There was only one difference. Lupus scribbled on his wax tablet.

'His skin was yellowish,' said Flavia, reading over Lupus's shoulder.

'Then it was definitely Mindius,' said Bato. 'He's got icterus.'

'What?' said Aristo. 'What's icterus?'

'Jaundice,' said Jonathan. 'It's a disease you get when you have too much yellow bile.'

Bato's soldier stopped before them and held out the tray. Bato waved his hand impatiently but Lupus took a beaker.

'Did the woman have a baby with her?' Nubia asked Lupus.

Lupus nodded as he drank, then mimed having a bundle on his front.

'That must have been Popo!' cried Flavia. 'And the woman was probably Lydia, his wet-nurse. But why did Mindius leave all these others and only take them?'

'I dread to think,' said Aristo.

'If we'd got here half an hour sooner,' cried Flavia, 'we could have saved Popo.'

'Sextus and Decimus are good men,' said Bato to Flavia. 'They'll rescue the baby before Mindius can do anything.' He automatically made the sign against evil.

Flavia nodded and fanned her hot face with her sunhat.

'What will happen to these children?' said Nubia to Bato. She was holding a little girl on her hip. Two more clung to her mustard-yellow tunic.

'Valerius Flaccus is on his way here with a carruca,' said Bato. 'He's going to process them and make sure they get back to their parents and homes.'

'Who?' said Flavia, and her heart seemed to stop. 'Valerius who?'

Bato gave her a distracted look; he was trying to reclaim a damp corner of his toga from little Gaius. 'Your friend, the young orator and poet. Gaius Valerius Flaccus. Your father convinced him to join our expedition, as well.'

'Floppy?' breathed Flavia, her heart now thudding like a drum. 'Here in Asia?' She and her friends all stared at Bato.

Bato allowed a half smile to cross his face. 'Yes,' he said. 'Gaius Valerius Flaccus is here in Asia. In fact, he's right behind you.'

Flavia turned to see a muscular young man standing

in the vestibule. He wore a cream tunic with two broad vertical red stripes, like Bato's. His straight dark hair flopped over his forehead and his mouth hung open as he gazed at her in utter astonishment.

'Floppy!' She dropped the hat and ran across the marble floor and threw her arms around him. 'Oh, Floppy! I can't believe you're here!'

For a wonderful moment she was hugging his slim warm waist and smelling his musky cinnamon body oil and hearing his heart thudding against her ear. But instead of greeting her in return, he took her gently by the shoulders and pushed her away. His hands were trembling and his face was very pale. 'Flavia Gemina,' he stammered. 'Is it really you? We all thought you were ... That is ...' He gestured stiffly towards two young women standing in the shadows behind him. 'Flavia, I'd like you to meet Prudentilla. My sponsa.'

SCROLL VIII

'Your sponsa?' Flavia stared in horror at Flaccus. 'Your *sponsa*?'

'Yes!' His deep voice had a strange tightness. 'Prudentilla is a senator's daughter. We were betrothed in July and we plan to marry in September.'

A dark-haired girl of sixteen or seventeen stepped forward with a smile. The woman behind her with downcast eyes was obviously her slave-girl. Lyncaeus was there, too: Flaccus's body slave. He was giving Flavia an encouraging smile, his eyebrows raised.

Flavia turned to Flaccus. 'But you ... when I ... I thought we ...' She could feel her face growing hotter and hotter.

Jonathan came to her rescue. 'Hello, Flaccus!' he said, coming up and adopting the boxer's stance. 'Keeping fit?' Jonathan made a false feint at the older youth and Flaccus smiled and pretended to parry Jonathan's blow.

Everyone laughed – a little too loudly – and now Aristo was stepping forward to greet Flaccus, and so were Nubia and Lupus.

While they were greeting one another and making introductions, Flavia studied Flaccus's fiancée. She was a classic Roman beauty: low forehead, long straight eyebrows above liquid brown eyes, a small mouth beneath a perfectly straight nose. Her dark hair was pinned up in a simple but elegant twist and she wore a leek green stola of the finest linen. Although she had just come in from the furnace-hot afternoon, she looked cool and fresh. Flavia felt a sickening lurch in the pit of her stomach.

'Prudentilla is going to help me look after the kidnapped children,' said Flaccus. 'She's very good with children. They love her.'

As if on cue, little Gaius detached himself from Bato's toga and went straight to Prudentilla. She knelt and whispered a few words to him, then stood and ruffled his hair. Gaius embraced her knees and gazed up at her with adoring eyes. Flaccus gave his betrothed an equally admiring look and Flavia's stomach lurched again. With a terrible certainty, she knew she was going to be sick.

'Excuse me,' she gasped. 'I'm just . . .'

And she ran out of the atrium in search of the latrines.

Nubia found Flavia bent over one of the holes in the polished marble bench of Mindius's three-seater latrine.

'Flavia?' whispered Nubia. 'I am so sorry.' She held out a goblet of posca. 'Drink this to refresh your mouth.'

Flavia lifted her face. She was a ghastly white and her skin had a sheen of sweat on it. 'Oh, Nubia,' she whispered. 'He's betrothed.'

'I know,' said Nubia. 'But you must come back and act as if nothing is bad. Otherwise they will come seeking you and ask many vexing questions.'

'I'm such a fool. I turned him down and now I've lost him for ever. I can't go back in there.'

Nubia put down the goblet, gripped Flavia's shoulders and pulled her almost roughly to her feet.

'You must come back,' said Nubia fiercely. 'You want to help those poor children who were taken from their homes. You want to find Miriam's baby, who must be sorely missing his beloved twin. You want to think about others and not yourself.'

'But ... but ...' Flavia's chin was trembling and her eyes brimming.

'Stop it!' hissed Nubia, and gave her friend a shake. 'Now is not the time to cry! Now is to be brave. That is what he admires about you. Be Flavia.'

'But I've lost him!'

'Yes. You have lost his love. But you do not want to lose his respect. Now drink this.'

Flavia took the goblet and drank, then wiped her mouth with the back of her hand. 'You're right.' She took a deep breath. 'I don't want to lose his respect.'

'Later you can cry,' said Nubia. 'But not now. Now we have a criminal mastermind to catch and a tiny baby to rescue.'

Flavia looked up in astonishment, then gave a sob of laughter. 'Oh, Nubia!' she cried. 'What would I do without you?'

'One hundred tetradrachms,' said Marcus Artorius Bato later that evening at dinner. He pushed a pile of silver coins across the table towards Aristo.

Jonathan and his friends had been to the baths before checking in to Chione's Hospitium, near the Eastern Gate, where Bato was staying. A boy had been dispatched to the *Ourania* to pick up their few belongings. Bato had convinced the landlady Chione to give them

Captain Geminus's old rooms. Now they all sat at a table on a balcony overlooking the circular harbour of Halicarnassus.

'Thank you,' said Aristo to Bato. He counted out five tetradrachms each for Jonathan and the others, then started to put the rest in his coin pouch. 'Captain Geminus will repay you as soon as he returns.'

'I'm counting on it,' said Bato drily. He was wearing his tunic but not his official toga.

'They won't all fit,' said Aristo, looking up from his coin purse.

Lupus held out his hand palm up and grinned.

Aristo smiled and shook his head. 'Thank you for the offer, Lupus, but I can put the rest in my travel bag.'

'That's the good news,' said Bato. 'The bad news is that Sextus and Decimus were not able to catch Mindius and the others.'

'Alas!' murmured Nubia. 'Poor Popo.'

'One disaster after another,' muttered Jonathan.

'Gustatio,' trilled a plump woman, sliding a platter of cheese-stuffed pastries onto the table. 'Isn't it the most beautiful evening?'

Something in her voice made Jonathan look up at her. It was a pleasant enough evening. Bats flitted in the lavender sky above and the temperature of the air was perfect. But her tone seemed to convey that it was the most beautiful day in the history of the world.

Bato opened his mouth to say something but the woman interrupted.

'Do you like the way I delivered that to you?' she asked.

'The service is excellent, as always, Chione,' said Bato.

'But did you see me come over here?' Chione persisted. 'Remember my limp?' Her round face almost glowed with happiness.

'Yes, I remember your limp.'

'But I don't anymore, do I?'

'If you say so. Could you bring some more of that nice apple tea?'

'Only if you watch me walk!'

'We'll watch.' Bato rolled his eyes but dutifully watched plump Chione walk back towards the kitchen door.

'Behold, she does not limp,' said Nubia.

Bato shrugged and turned back to them. 'One of my soldiers was interrogating the kitchen slaves,' he said. 'Apparently Mindius had a house in Ephesus.'

'What is effy sis?' asked Nubia.

'It's a sea port about eighty miles north of here,' said Bato. 'It's the biggest, richest city in the province of Asia.'

'And Mindius has a house there?' asked Aristo. 'As well as his estate here?'

'Yes,' said Bato, 'And not only does he have estates here and in Ephesus, but he also has property in Ostia.'

'Of course!' said Jonathan. 'I knew his name was familiar. There are some members of the Mindius clan at the synagogue in Ostia.'

Lupus wrote something on his wax tablet and held it up. NO HOUSEHOLD SHRINE. JEWISH?

Bato raised both eyebrows. 'Correct. It took us a few days to work that out. Yes, Mindius is indeed Jewish. I intend to visit the Ostian branch of his clan when I return. In the meantime, I have decided to sail to Ephesus by ship. I suspect that's where Mindius was heading when Lupus saw him riding away.'

'With big Ursus and the tiny baby?' asked Nubia.

'Yes.'

'What can we do?' asked Aristo. 'What can we do to help?'

Jonathan looked over at Flavia, this was the sort of question she usually asked. But Flavia was staring bleakly at her plate, her food untouched.

'You and the children,' said Bato, 'can help Flaccus find the names and places of origin of the children, so we can return them to their families. They're all staying at the tetrarch's villa; Flaccus and his sponsa are there, too. Apparently Flaccus's father knew the tetrarch.'

Nubia frowned, 'What is tet ark?' she asked.

'Tetrarch,' corrected Bato: 'the local official.' He turned back to Aristo. 'We need to know who these children are, where they're from, how old they are now and how old they were when they were captured. Also, whether they were freeborn or sold as slaves. You'll need to help Flaccus write letters to the families. If any children can't remember their families or are too young, write detailed descriptions.' He smiled at Flavia. 'An observant girl like you should be particularly good at that part.'

Flavia did not look up from her plate. Bato's smile became a puzzled frown. 'Flavia Gemina,' he said. 'I've sent word to your father, telling him that you and your friends are alive and well. I'm sure he'll be rushing back here to see you.'

'Thank you,' said Flavia quietly, but did not look up from her untouched dinner.

Bato caught Jonathan's eye. He raised his pale eyebrows quickly and dropped them, as if to say: Well, I tried. He cleared his throat, but before he could speak,

Chione plonked a pitcher of fragrant apple tea on the table.

'Oh, if only you could have been in the theatre today!' She said. 'That prophet is amazing. He preached the gospel.'

'What is god spell?' asked Nubia.

'Why, the Good News!' said Chione. 'Gospel means good news. He told lots of wonderful stories about miracles and god's love and this man called Jesus who died and then came alive again.'

Jonathan stiffened. 'The prophet is a Christian?'

Chione shrugged happily. 'No idea. All I know is that I used to limp and now I don't. I don't know what you call that, but I call it good news.'

In his vision he is flying above the land. Far below, the hills are the golden folds of a velvet blanket, the rivers are ribbons, the lakes are drops of molten silver. On a dusty thread of road he sees three horses, four souls. The horses are small as ants from this height, but his eyes are eagle-sharp and he can see their flaring nostrils, their eyelashes, the foam on their flanks. He can see the riders, too. A giant of a man with a wild expression. An older man, grim and determined. And a young woman, with the baby still at her breast. Three horses. Four souls. And one of them is the Key to a great battle in the constellation of the Maiden.

SCROLL IX

The next morning the tetrarch's secretary led Flavia and her friends through various frescoed rooms and marbled corridors to an inner courtyard lined with green spiral columns. Flavia saw Flaccus at once, standing over his slave Lyncaeus, who was writing something at a marble-topped table. A large carpet had been spread on the ground and on it sat two dozen children, painfully thin, but bathed and clean and playing happily.

'Alas!' said Nubia. 'The poor children are sitting on carpet like the ones they weave with wounded fingers. This is very cruel.'

Aristo nodded grimly. 'I'll mention it to Bato.'

Prudentilla and her slave-girl were moving among the children. Each of the boys had a wooden horse and every girl had a wooden jointed doll with coloured woollen hair and a matching tunic.

A little girl tugged Flavia's hand and said in Greek: 'See my doll?'

Flavia glanced down. It was Salome, the sallow-skinned girl with dark hair. Flavia gave the little girl a smile then looked back at Prudentilla.

Nubia bent to examine Salome's doll. 'It is charming,' said Nubia in Greek. She sat gracefully on the carpet between Salome and Flavilla.

'The dolls were Prudentilla's idea,' said Flaccus, coming up to Flavia with a smile. 'She bought them in the market yesterday. Thank you for coming,' he added. 'It will make our job much easier.'

Flavia knew his eyes were on her but she couldn't bear to meet his gaze; instead, she pretended to watch two boys playing with their horses.

'Flavia,' he said, his voice low. 'Don't be angry with me for asking her to marry me. Word reached us in June that you were dead and besides, didn't you take a vow to remain a maiden for ever? Prudentilla is a wonderful woman. I know you'll like her.'

Flavia looked up into his dark eyes, so full of tenderness and concern. Half a dozen different emotions bubbled up inside her: frustration, anger, love, jealousy, confusion and longing. Tears were welling, too.

'Flavia,' he said huskily, and took a step towards her. But before he could add anything Prudentilla came up behind him, smiling sweetly.

'Hello, Flavia!' she said. 'Hello, Jonathan, Nubia and Lupus. Aristo.'

Prudentilla's cheeks were flushed and she looked very pretty in a rose coloured stola with a matching necklace of tiny pink pearls and gold beads. Flavia noticed she was also wearing a gold betrothal ring on the fourth finger of her left hand; it was exactly like the ring Flaccus had once offered her, showing two right hands clasped.

'Here,' said Prudentilla, handing a doll to Nubia and a wooden horse each to Jonathan and Lupus. Then she held out a doll to Flavia. 'And this one is for you.'

Flavia made no move to take the doll. 'I'm not a child,' she said. 'I am twelve years old now and of a marriageable age.' She darted Flaccus a look.

Prudentilla's brown eyes were wide. 'Are you of marriageable age now? I thought you'd taken a vow never to marry. At least that's what Gaius told me.'

'Maybe I've changed my mind,' said Flavia.

A flash of alarm passed across Prudentilla's pretty face, but she recovered quickly and shrugged. 'Anyway,' she added, 'you needn't be ashamed to use these. They are much more than toys.'

'Are they?' said Flavia coldly.

'Yes,' said Prudentilla. 'If you ask a frightened child a direct question, they're often afraid to speak to you. But if your toy horse or doll asks their doll or horse a question, they will tell you many things.'

'Giving them dolls is very wise,' said Nubia from her place on the carpet between Flavilla and Salome. Her doll had mustard-yellow hair and tunic and she was already making it walk over to greet the girls' dolls.

'Try it,' said Flaccus gently. 'It really does work.'

Reluctantly, Flavia took her doll from Prudentilla. It had a blue tunic and pale blue hair.

'What we're doing,' continued Flaccus, 'is trying to find out as much as we can about each child. Then we write down what we learn on a piece of papyrus, one sheet per child. There are pens and ink and papyrus on that table over there. Pick a child who hasn't had a sheet filled out, talk to them.' Here he smiled at Lupus. 'Or just listen to them chatter, and write down anything which might be important. We've managed to get all their names, but we still need information like their ages, home towns, family name, how they were kidnapped and how long they've been in captivity.'

'I can help you record their details, if you like,' said Aristo to Flaccus.

'Yes, please. Oh, Jonathan. Little Joseph over there speaks Aramaic. Can you interview him?'

'Of course.' Jonathan looked up from examining his toy horse.

Flaccus led Jonathan and Lupus over to where some of the boys were playing. Aristo joined Lyncaeus at the table.

Prudentilla caught Flavia's free hand. 'Come!' she said. 'Let's talk to little Agatha here.'

Prudentilla's fingers were cool and slightly moist. Flavia snatched her hand away as if it had been burnt. Prudentilla smiled, but the flush on her cheeks deepened.

'Here's Agatha,' she said, sitting gracefully beside a dark-haired Greek girl. 'We think she came from one of the islands, but we don't know which one.'

Flavia sat facing Flaccus's wife-to-be and the little girl.

'Hello!' she made her doll say in Greek. 'I'm Flavia Gemina.'

'Hello.' Agatha's doll replied timidly in Greek.

'I'm from Ostia in Italia,' said Flavia's doll. 'Where are you from?'

'Oh, Flavia!' giggled Prudentilla. 'You speak Greek with an Egyptian accent!'

Flavia swallowed hard and said in Latin. 'That's because we've just spent two months in Egypt.'

'That explains why you're so tanned. I would rather die than be seen with such brown skin. And your hair is so short. It barely touches your shoulders. Is that the way the women wear their hair in Alexandria?'

'No,' said Flavia in Latin. 'I cut off my hair to offer it to Neptune as a thanks offering.' She turned back to Agatha and made her doll speak in Greek. 'I have a dog

64

called Scuto. He's far away in Italia. I miss him very much.'

'I don't have a dog,' said Agatha's doll. 'But I would love a puppy.'

'Gaius has told me all about you,' said Prudentilla to Flavia. She was still speaking Latin. 'He told me he proposed to you.'

Flavia ignored Prudentilla. 'My friend Nubia found some puppies in the graveyard once,' she made her doll say in Greek.

'The man on the beach told me he'd lost his puppy,' said Agatha's doll. 'He asked me to help him look for it.'

'I'm not jealous of you in the least,' said Prudentilla. 'Gaius told me he was glad you rejected him.'

Flavia couldn't ignore this: 'He was glad I said no?'

'Yes. You see, he only proposed on impulse.'

'He said that?' Flavia felt sick.

Prudentilla nodded sweetly.

Agatha made her doll speak again: 'The man said his puppy was on the boat. I went on the boat and looked everywhere but there was no puppy.'

Prudentilla continued speaking in Latin: 'Apparently,' she said, 'all Gaius's friends were getting betrothed or married and he didn't want to feel left out. You were the first person he thought of.' She smiled. 'He assures me he never really loved you. He was just in love with the idea of being married!'

'That was the last time I saw mummy and daddy,' said Agatha, her lower lip quivering. 'And I miss them.'

'After all,' said Prudentilla, admiring her betrothal ring. 'How could Gaius possibly love you? You're not even a woman yet, whereas I am. No, I'm not jealous one bit.'

Flavia stood up, threw down her doll, and ran out of the courtyard.

Jonathan and Aristo found Flavia pacing the atrium of the tetrarch's villa.

Jonathan sighed. 'At last! We've been looking for you everywhere.'

'Have you been crying?' Aristo asked.

'No!' said Flavia angrily.

'Come back to the courtyard, Flavia,' said Jonathan. 'Help us help the children.'

'I can't!' said Flavia. 'I can't be in the same place as them.'

'You can't be in the same place as whom?' asked Aristo.

'As *him*! And her.' Flavia glared at him with red-rimmed eyes. 'I hate him!'

Aristo frowned in puzzlement.

Jonathan rolled his eyes at his tutor. 'You have no idea what she means,' he said. 'Do you?'

'No,' said Aristo. 'I have no idea what Flavia means.'

Nubia and Lupus came hurrying into the atrium.

'Behold! You are here,' said Nubia.

Lupus lifted his upturned hands to the ceiling and raised his eyebrows, as if to say 'Why?'

'Yes, Flavia,' said Aristo. 'Why did you bolt like that?'

Jonathan folded his arms across his chest and tipped his head on one side. 'Flavia's in love with Flaccus,' he said to Aristo. 'And she can't bear to see him with Prudentilla.'

Flavia rounded on him. 'I don't love him. I hate him!'

Jonathan nodded. 'Of course you do. You hate him because you love him. *Odi et amo*, as Catullus says.'

Aristo looked at Flavia in disbelief. 'You? In love? But you've only just turned twelve,' he said. 'You're too young to be in love.'

'No, we're not!' cried both girls, and Flavia added: 'We're both of marriageable age now.'

'By Apollo!' muttered Aristo, looking from Flavia to Nubia. 'I suppose you are. I'm so used to thinking of you as children.'

'We're not children,' said Flavia vehemently. 'And even if we don't want to get married right away, we can still be in love.'

'Both of you?' said Aristo. He looked at Nubia in surprise. 'You're both in love?'

'Yes,' said Jonathan. 'Both of them.'

At this, Nubia gave Jonathan such a fierce look of warning that he took a step back.

'You boys also?' said Aristo after a short pause. 'Are you also in love?'

'Master of the Universe, no!' said Jonathan.

Lupus shook his head vigorously and pretended to vomit.

Aristo nodded thoughtfully and looked at Nubia. 'So it's only you two girls I have to worry about?'

Both girls were glaring at Jonathan, so he kept quiet.

'Well, well, well,' said Aristo, with a tight smile. 'Lucky Flaccus, to have so many admirers.'

'I don't admire him!' cried Flavia. 'I told you: I hate him! I can't be in the same room as him and I can't stay here in Halicarnassus doing nothing when Mindius is escaping.'

'We're not doing nothing,' said Jonathan. 'We're trying to reunite kidnapped children with their parents.'

'Prudentilla and Flaccus can do that perfectly well

67

without us,' said Flavia. 'And every moment we stay here, Biggest Buyer is taking my baby cousin further and further away.'

'He's my nephew,' said Jonathan. 'I care about him, too.'

'Bato will catch Mindius,' said Aristo. 'He'll be waiting for him in Ephesus.'

Flavia rounded on Aristo. 'How can you be so sure? Bato told us his two soldiers would catch Mindius, but they didn't. And what if Mindius isn't really going to Ephesus? Or what if he changes his mind halfway? Or what if Bato's ship sinks,' – Flavia made the sign against evil – 'and he never gets there?'

Jonathan nodded. 'Flavia's right,' he said. 'There are a hundred things that could go wrong with Bato's plan.'

'We're going to catch Biggest Buyer ourselves,' said Flavia, 'and save Miriam's baby. I've got it all planned. We'll take some of those horses we saw at Mindius's villa and we'll start for Ephesus today.' She looked at Aristo. 'You can't stop us, so you may as well come with us.'

Aristo stared back. 'But I . . . we've never been to this province before,' he stuttered. 'It could be dangerous.'

'It could be very dangerous,' said Flavia, and Jonathan saw that her eyes had a bright, almost feverish gleam. 'But the stakes are high and it's worth the risk.' As she turned to go, Jonathan heard her mutter to herself: 'He told me he loved my courage . . . I'll prove I'm braver than she is.'

SCROLL X

They left Halicarnassus around noon, riding on five of Mindius's finest horses. Nubia was in the lead. She sat upon a magnificent black stallion that nobody else had dared to mount.

Aristo had used some of Bato's loan to buy provisions. They were wearing light, long-sleeved linen tunics and wide-brimmed straw hats to protect them from the merciless sun. Nubia and her three friends carried travellers' baskets bought cheap in the market. Each basket contained a hooded woollen cloak, a spare tunic, a comb and a bath-set. Aristo had his leather travelling satchel with his lyre in it. He had also bought a gourd of water for each of them, and two hemp bags of sunflower seeds to stave off hunger on the road.

Nubia had prepared enough horse feed for two days: a mix of barley, beans, fenugreek and vetch. She had learned how to make it in the stables of the Greens in Rome: it was especially good for stamina and endurance. She had also packed two of Prudentilla's dolls: the one with yellow hair and the one with blue hair. She and Flavia were both dressed as boys, to discourage trouble. When in Egypt, Nubia had learned to walk like a boy, stomping rather than gliding, and pretending to be confident. But riding this stallion she didn't need to pretend: on his back, she felt powerful and brave.

'Heracleia, twenty-five miles,' called Jonathan from the rear. He was looking at a milestone. 'Ephesus, eighty-five.'

They left the town and its tombs behind, the road always ascending. Nubia felt the horse's muscles ripple as he effortlessly took the slope. The whole world throbbed with cicadas and the rhythmic clopping of hooves. She could smell the heady scent of thyme and the pungent aroma of horse. Despite the tragic cause of their quest, a bittersweet joy flooded her heart. She was with her friends and with her beloved Aristo.

'What are you naming your horse, Flavia?' asked Nubia, reining in her stallion so that Flavia could come abreast. 'I am calling mine Tarquin. It is the name of a king of Rome but also reminds me of my brother Taharqo, like the horse.'

Flavia looked down at her strawberry roan gelding and sighed. 'I suppose I'll call mine Herodotus.' She gave a small smile. 'Because he comes from Halicarnassus.'

'Good choice,' said Aristo with a smile. 'I'll call my little grey mare Calliope. Her hooves are very musical and she clips along like a verse of Homer.'

Nubia smiled, too, and looked over her shoulder at Jonathan.

'Mine's as sluggish as the Tiber river,' he grumbled from the rear. 'And about the same colour, too.'

'Call her Tiberina,' said Aristo, and winked at Nubia.

'What about you, Lupus?' said Nubia happily. 'What are you naming your pretty little bay mare?'

'Unnnggh!' said Lupus cheerfully, and they all laughed.

As the road climbed, the air grew cooler and the scent

of pines mingled with the spicy fragrance of the maquis. Sometimes the scenery reminded Nubia of Greece and at other times it might have been Italia, but then she would catch the strong scent of thyme and remember: they were in Asia, thyme-scented Asia.

It was afternoon and there were few other travellers on the road. Of those they met, none remembered seeing three riders, one of whom was a giant on a black gelding.

'They're a day ahead of us,' remarked Aristo. 'I'd be surprised if someone travelling today had seen them.'

Once a snake slithered across the road and Nubia's horse reared up. But she calmed him with soothing words and a pat on the neck.

'You ride very well,' said Aristo, coming up along side. 'When did you learn?'

'I learned when I was young,' she said. 'I can ride camel, too.'

'I'm impressed. You know, you've changed a lot in half a year. Your Latin is much better and your Greek is nearly perfect.'

'I was in Egypt for two months,' she said. 'Everyone is speaking Greek there.'

'Still, you picked it up quickly.'

'I am having a good teacher,' she said softly.

'And you're a talented girl,' he said. 'I mean: a talented young lady.'

Nubia glanced at him. Because his mare was a little smaller than Tarquin, her eyes were level with his. She always felt powerful and strong on horseback and now she smiled and looked ahead again. She knew he was still looking at her and she felt her cheeks grow hot.

As they reached the highest point of the pass, a sea

breeze ruffled her tunic and cooled her face. Down below, she glimpsed turquoise water between the dark-green pine trees.

Aristo slowed Calliope, so Nubia reined in Tarquin, too. The others came up beside them and, as the hoof beats ceased, Nubia could hear the soporific pulse of the cicadas, the breeze in her ears and the distant clank of goat bells.

'Thalassa! Thalassa!' quoted Aristo. 'The sea! The sea!'

Nubia remembered the quote from one of their lessons and she smiled. 'Xenophon,' she said, and felt his admiring gaze again. She urged Tarquin forward with her heels, and they continued down the winding road, catching glimpses of secluded bays to their left, between the pines.

'I'm starving,' called Jonathan from the rear an hour later. 'Shall we have some of those sunflower seeds?'

Aristo pointed. 'That looks like a tavern down there in the shade of those pines,' he called over his shoulder. 'Let's water the horses and have a rest and something to eat in the shade.'

But when they reached the roadside tavern, the inn-keeper came out shaking his head.

'Sorry,' he said in Greek. 'You can water your horses in my brook and sit on my benches, but I don't have a scrap of food to offer you. That prophet and his people came through here late yesterday afternoon. Ate every crumb in my house. It was like a flock of locusts. Are you hoping to catch up with him?' he added, as Nubia and her friends dismounted.

'Actually,' said Aristo, 'we're pursuing a young woman

and a baby, travelling with a distinguished-looking man and a big body-slave.'

'Oh, you mean Mindius!' said the man. He turned his head and spat onto the dusty ground.

'You know about Mindius?' asked Flavia.

'Everybody in this region knows about him,' said the innkeeper. 'He and his little entourage came by yesterday, too. Not long after the prophet and his crowd. Perhaps they want to be healed!'

'I doubt it,' said Aristo drily.

'Did Mindius say where he was going?' asked Flavia.

'Didn't say anything at all,' said the man. 'They rode straight through as if an entire legion were on their heels.'

The road descended as they left the coast and presently they were in a flat, fertile river valley, full of vineyards and fruit trees. Late in the afternoon, the terrain became hilly again, and Lupus and his friends passed an ancient citadel as the town was coming to life after the siesta. They stopped at a caupona to water the horses, and beneath the shaded awning Lupus drank a salted yogurt drink while the others snacked on green almonds washed down with sour cherry juice.

The yawning serving-girl did not remember seeing Mindius, but she told them that the prophet had passed through at midday. He had wanted to camp outside of town, but the village elders had chased him out and couldn't they see the mess his followers had made?

'Still,' she said. 'It wasn't all bad. Some of his followers were selling these handkerchiefs. They've been touched by the healer himself. I got myself one of the last ones.' She opened a blue silk scarf to show them a small scrap of unbleached linen within. 'This cost me a tetra-drachm,' she said, 'but I don't mind. I'm going to give it to my old granny. She's not well.'

Lupus stretched his hand towards the scrap of cloth and grunted, as if to say: May I see it?

'What's he want?' said the girl, folding up the blue scarf with the magic handkerchief safely inside.

'I think he just wants to look at it,' said Flavia. 'Right, Lupus?'

He nodded and reached out again.

'No you don't!' The serving girl tucked the blue scarf down the front of her tunic. 'If you touch it the power goes out of it.'

Lupus hung his head and tried to look pathetic but the girl's resolve did not waver.

But when they mounted their horses again, Lupus was so hopeful about catching up with the healing prophet that he found his mare's jouncing almost bearable. Finally, at dusk, they overtook the prophet and his crowds on a forested hillside just beyond Euromus.

There were perhaps two hundred people with the prophet, scattered among the pine trees of the slope. Beside some trees near the road stood horses and carts and even a camel. Several people were setting up make-shift tents.

'Come hear the prophet!' a woman called out to them, and it seemed to Lupus that she was looking directly at him. 'Come hear Tychicus! He's preaching the good news. He heals the sick and gives sight to the blind!'

Lupus reined in his little mare and looked for the prophet called Tychicus. He thought he could see him at the very top of the slope, in a clearing among the pines: a stocky, bearded man in a turban and long blue tunic. The people around the man were sitting quietly and listening, those on the periphery were lying down, chatting, even preparing food.

Could the prophet really heal the sick and make the blind see? Could he make the dumb talk? Could he heal Lupus?

Jonathan had turned Tiberina; now he brought her up beside him. 'Aristo and Flavia say we should press on,' said Jonathan in a low voice. 'Aristo says his map shows a tavern with stables at the port of Heracleia at the foot of Mount Latmus. It's not far but we need to get there before dark. I'm sorry,' he added. 'I'd like to hear the prophet, too, but we—'

Lupus angrily kicked his horse into motion; he knew what Jonathan was going to say.

Jonathan felt bad about hurrying Lupus, but he had worries of his own. The voice in his head was becoming more and more insistent, perhaps because there were no distractions while riding on horseback, just the incessant throb of the cicadas and the clopping of horses' hooves.

They reached Heracleia at lamp-lighting time. It was a small port town at the foot of a granite mountain studded with strange tortured boulders. They found Endymion's Tavern just outside the southern wall, and ate a spicy dinner of goat stew and flatbread.

The landlord had not seen Mindius pass by, but because they were the only guests he lingered beside their table to complain about the mosquitoes and business falling off due to the harbour silting up and how the prophet and his hoards would descend on them the following day.

'Lucky you got here when you did,' he said. 'They'll be swarming like flies on a carcass tomorrow. I hope they pay.' Jonathan didn't mind the man's chatter. When he was talking the voice was silent.

Now the landlord was telling them that his name was Endymion, after the handsome and mythical shepherd loved by the moon goddess Selene.

'Can you see the resemblance?' he asked, wiggling dark eyebrows that met above his nose.

Jonathan snorted but Nubia nodded politely. Lupus and Flavia were too preoccupied to respond.

'Legend has it,' said Endymion, 'that my namesake still sleeps his magic sleep in one of the caves up there on Mount Latmus.'

After dinner, Aristo improvised a song about Endymion while Nubia accompanied him on her flute.

The landlord was so moved by their music that he offered them a special rate on their room.

This room turned out to be a dormitory with eight straw mattresses on an earthen floor. It smelt faintly of urine because there was a vespasian in the corner and only one small window. At least there were no other travellers, so they had the room to themselves.

Jonathan kicked off his sandals and lay down on his bed. It was dark now, and despite the heat and mosquitoes and prickly mattresses, the others fell asleep at once.

But the voice in his head would not allow him any rest. Since they had left Halicarnassus it had grown stronger. And the more he tried to ignore it, the more it persisted. Now the voice spoke to him clearly, in a sneering tone:

It's your fault. It's all your fault. If you hadn't gone

to Rome your family would be fine. Had to look for your mother, didn't you? And what good did it do? It's all your fault. Stupid. Stupid. Stupid. You killed them. Burned them. Men. Women. Babies. Your fault. All your fault.

Jonathan rolled onto his side and wrapped the greasy pillow around his head. But the voice was inside his head, not outside, and this did not help. The previous night it had woken him at the darkest hour with an insistent thought. **You deserve to burn. You deserve to burn. Burn in fire. Burn in fire. Burn. Burn. Burn.**

Now the straw in the mattress was making him wheeze and a mosquito was whining peevishly, so he stood up, shook out his cloak, wrapped it around his face and lay on the packed earth floor. He closed his eyes and tried to relax. His muscles were stiff from riding and he was having trouble sucking enough breath into his lungs. Even above his own wheezing he could hear the voice taunting him again: **You're pathetic. Can't even breathe. Can't breathe. Why don't you just die? You're pathetic.**

Hot tears of self-pity spilled out and for a short time he indulged them. But then the voice began calling him a '**pathetic cry-baby**', so he got up and slipped out of the room and onto the wooden colonnaded walkway with its view of the mountain looming behind the stables. A nearly full moon made the strange barren rocks on the mountain look like crouching giants. Jonathan found a battered wicker rocking chair in the colonnade. It creaked softly as he sat down in it. The night was warm and smelled faintly of stagnant water. From the south came the textured singing of frogs in the marshy salt flats. A million stars throbbed in the sky

77

above, attending the moon. Over to the west, above the sea, Jonathan could see the constellation of Leo, Nubia's birth sign. Beside it was Virgo the Maiden. Whenever he imagined filaments of light connecting the stars of Virgo, the lines seemed to describe a squarish body with arms raised high and legs kicking out. It always made him think of a falling figure, more warrior than maiden. He had been born under that sign of the Zodiac, and it reminded him that in a month he would be thirteen and officially a man.

Even if you live to be that old, sneered the voice, **you'll never be a man. Just a coward. A coward who deserves to die**.

Jonathan dug his fingernails into his scalp, squeezed his eyes shut and tried not to scream.

If he had been looking, he would have seen a small figure emerge from the inky-shadowed colonnade and run silently across the moonlit courtyard towards the stables.

But Jonathan's eyes were closed and he did not see Lupus.

—

SCROLL XI

Lupus had waited until the others were asleep.

But now the moon was up and he used its light to creep out of the dormitory and across the deserted courtyard to the stables. The night was warm, the air thick and damp. Frogs croaked sleepily in the nearby marshes and mosquitoes whined around his ears.

Inside the stables the air was hot and humid, heavy with the pungent scent of hay, leather and horse dung. One of the horses snuffled softly. It was the little bay mare he had been riding. She had put in a long day and he felt sorry for her.

He stroked her flank and hummed softly. If he could have spoken, he would have whispered comforting words to her. He would have told her that they were only going a few miles south to the prophet's camp. He would have told her that he was going to touch something much more powerful than a holy handkerchief. He was going to touch the prophet himself. If he could have spoken, he would have told the bay mare that this was one of the most important journeys he would ever make, because it might end with his healing.

But he could not speak so he contented himself with humming and grunting as he saddled and mounted her.

As he set out along the dusty, moon-washed road, he

allowed himself a moment of self-pity. His friends would never really know what it felt like not to have a tongue. They would never know how dry his mouth was every morning, how every bite threatened to choke him, how humiliating it was to sound like an idiot each time he tried to speak.

The little bay mare moved slowly up the silver road, her hooves muffled by the thick layer of dust and by the soporific creak of frogs in the marshes to his right. Lupus was tired. The warmth of the night and the rhythmic pace made him drowsy. He allowed his head to droop onto his chest.

For a moment he dreamt there was something hot and wet and alive in his mouth, choking him, suffocating him. Lupus woke with a start, his heart thumping against his ribs. It had only been a dream, and he breathed easier, raised his waterskin and squirted some water into his tongueless mouth.

After a mile or two, a low ground mist began to swirl around the mare's legs and her nostrils flared as she caught a whiff of something unpleasant. He smelt it, too: the faint scent of bad cheese and sulphur. Lupus was wide awake now.

The moon painted the road and shrubs in silver, but the shadows in the oaks on the hillside to his left were inky black. A single oak tree by the side of the road seemed to stretch out its branches towards him, like twisted grasping arms. Despite the warm night, Lupus shuddered. He sensed the mare's unease, too.

Suddenly a head emerged from the mist at the side of the road.

Lupus stared in horror. The creature had horns and evil yellow eyes, but apart from that it was invisible. Was it a wild animal? Or some kind of demon?

Terrified, the mare reared up with a squeal and pawed the air with her hoofs. Lupus felt himself slipping from the horse's back and as he fell towards the stony ground he cried out for help.

Then darkness enveloped him and he knew no more.

In his vision he sees a man healed of demons.

The prophet puts his hand on the man's head and speaks the Name with authority. Dark shapes twist and coil out of the man's belly and slither away into the dry grasses, they fall from his neck and shoulders like leeches burnt with flame, they detach themselves from his scalp and whirr up into the sky like locusts. Exhausted, the man collapses onto the earth, as one dead. Presently the sobs of relief and the tears of regret show that he is still alive.

Jonathan was the first to see Lupus limp into the courtyard of the Endymion Tavern at dawn the next morning.

'Lupus! What happened?' Jonathan hurriedly stuffed his cloak into his travelling basket and ran to his friend. Nubia and Aristo were just leading the horses out of the stables. They ran to Lupus, too, and Flavia followed them.

'Behold!' said Nubia softly. 'You are covered in wounds.'

Lupus hung his head and did not reply. His mare – still saddled – was last out of the stables. Now she came up to Lupus and snorted softly, almost apologetically.

'Let me have a look,' said Jonathan to Lupus. 'Let me see your arms.'

Lupus dutifully held out his arms. His face was grubby and tear-streaked.

'These are just scratches,' said Jonathan. 'They should heal quickly. We just need to sponge them regularly with vinegar.' He looked around for the innkeeper.

'Did you fall off the horse?' asked Flavia.

Lupus nodded miserably.

'You'll have some bad bruises then,' said Jonathan. 'I can try to find some wall-nettle to make a paste which I can put on the places that hurt.'

Lupus shrugged.

'What possessed you to go out in the middle of the night?' asked Aristo. 'There are robbers and wild animals and potholes which could trip up your horse . . . Is that what happened?'

Lupus continued to stare at the hard-packed earth of the courtyard.

'Did you try to see prophet who heals?' asked Nubia softly.

'Of course!' cried Flavia. 'That's where you went.'

Jonathan felt a pang of guilt; he should have guessed.

'Did you see him?' asked Nubia. 'Was he there?'

'It's obvious he never reached him,' said Jonathan.

'Oh, poor Lupus!' whispered Flavia.

Lupus gave her a ferocious glare, then jerked his head towards the road, as if to say: Let's go.

'What?' said Jonathan. 'No vinegar for your scratches? No wall-nettle paste for your bruises?

Lupus shook his head and used the edge of the water trough to climb onto the little bay mare.

Jonathan sighed and mounted his own horse. He was beginning to wheeze again and the voice was back, reminding him that all these bad things were his fault.

★

They left Heracleia as the sun was rising, and a short time later passed a flock of long-haired black goats. Some of the goats stopped and stared up at them with malevolent eyes: yellow with a black slit for a pupil. Nubia shuddered and was surprised to hear Lupus give a bitter laugh.

The morning was still relatively cool and the flat river valley seemed like a paradise to Nubia. The landscape was a patchwork of emerald-green vineyards, silver-green olives and pale-gold barley, punctuated here and there by the tall dark flame-shaped cypress trees, with a backdrop of lavender foothills and blue mountains beyond. The road was new, built in Vespasian's time, but they preferred to use the dusty verge of the road. That way they could easily pass a slow-moving wagon and let fast-riding imperial messengers through. Also, Nubia knew that with unshod hooves the horses preferred the soft verge to the metalled road.

At noon they crossed the River Maeander, a wide, slow-moving river with lush reeds and grass on either side. An hour later they crossed it again.

'This river is famous,' remarked Aristo, 'because it winds back and forth like a snake. I suppose you could say it meanders along.'

Nubia nodded and smiled at him. Then she looked at Flavia. Usually, a fact like this would interest her. But Flavia, Jonathan and Lupus were all staring miserably ahead. It hurt her heart to see her friends unhappy and she wished there was something she could do.

She pulled her flute out from beneath the neck of her tunic and began to play a cheerful song, but this attracted the attention of a farmer and his slaves in a slow-moving cart, and Aristo frowned and motioned for her to stop.

'We don't want to draw attention to ourselves,' he said, when the cart was out of earshot. He gave her a sad smile. 'And your music is unforgettable.'

When they stopped mid-afternoon to pick sun-warmed grapes from the roadside vines and drink warm sweet water from their gourds, Nubia saw her friends revive a little. But as soon as they mounted their horses they fell back into their miserable silence. Nubia gently kicked Tarquin with her heels, so that he trotted forward to ride abreast with Aristo.

Her tutor rode very well and she felt a sudden surge of pride and longing as she looked at him. The column of his neck was as smooth and flawless as bronze, and there was something about the curve of his cheekbones and his eyelashes that made her heart hurt. She longed to reach out and touch his face.

'What is it?' he gave her his heart-stopping smile.

'You ride very well, too,' she said shyly.

'Do you want me to tell you why?' he asked, with a quick sidelong glance. 'How I learned to ride in Corinth when I was eight?'

'Yes,' said Nubia softly. 'Tell me everything about your growing up.'

SCROLL XII

For the rest of her life, Nubia would remember the first time she saw Ephesus. They had crested a mountain and the city lay below them, two or three miles distant. From here it looked like a scattering of coloured tesserae at the foot of golden hills. A river flowed to the north of the city walls, into the sea. A man-made channel connected a harbour to this river, just where it met the sea. A ship was sailing up the canal to the harbour even as she watched.

In the foreground, the pine-covered mountain slopes glowed emerald green in the late afternoon light. Birds were singing, the breeze was cool, the soft air smelt of dust and incense. The pulsing of the cicadas was like a heartbeat. There was a presence here: a sadness mixed with joy, a poignant hopefulness. Unaccountably, Nubia's eyes brimmed with tears.

'Do you feel that?' she said.

'Feel what?' grumbled Flavia. 'I can't feel anything. Especially not my bottom. It's numb.'

Nubia glanced to her right, towards Jonathan and Lupus. Both looked tired and miserable.

'I feel it,' said Aristo, pulling up his grey mare on her left. 'This place is special.' He turned to look at Nubia. 'It feels like . . . coming home.'

And she saw that his eyelashes glistened with tears.

As they rode down out of the pine-clad mountains toward Ephesus, a honeybee buzzed around Lupus's face. He swatted angrily.

'Don't harm that bee,' said Aristo.

Lupus grunted: Why not?

'It's a symbol of Ephesus. The goddess Artemis is worshipped here, and her followers are called "bees". Also, Ephesus is famous for its thyme-flavoured honey. Finally, according to legend, some bees led Prince Androclus to this place.'

Aristo looked expectantly at Flavia, but she remained silent.

'Who was Prince Androclus?' asked Nubia.

Lupus saw him give Nubia a grateful glance. 'Androclus was a prince of Athens, an Ionian.'

'What is eye own knee on?'

'The Greeks from Athens were descended from a man called Ion,' said Aristo. 'And called themselves Ionians. Several of them left Athens and came to colonise this part of Asia: henceforth known as Ionia. Androclus was one of those who set out to found a new city. One legend says that the Muses, disguised as bees, led him here. Another story says that a fish and a boar led the way.'

'A fish and a boar?' At last Flavia's interest was aroused.

'Yes. An oracle had told Androclus that a boar and a fish would show him where to settle. One day he and his men arrived on the banks of the Little Maeander – the river to the north of the city – and found the natives roasting freshly-caught fish over open fires.'

'All this talk of honey and boar and fish is making me hungry,' said Jonathan.

Lupus nodded his agreement.

Aristo pointed towards the city lying before them. 'As Androclus and his band of men approached the people cooking their catch, a piece of fish fell off its spit, scattering sparks from the fire and setting a nearby bush on fire. Out of the bush burst a wild boar, terrified by the flames.'

Lupus gave a grudging snort of laughter.

'Androclus speared the boar on the slopes of Mount Coressus, and he and his men feasted on it. And so,' concluded Aristo, 'they knew this place was ordained for them.'

The bee was still buzzing around Lupus's head but something more ominous had caught his attention. They were nearing the first tombs outside Ephesus now, and two crosses stood facing each other on either side of the road.

The one on the right still bore the mouldering remains of its victim. Even from a distance Lupus could see the body had been picked at by birds and wild animals. The feet were still nailed in place but both lower leg bones were missing.

Lupus grunted and pointed at the other cross. It was empty.

'Behold, one is empty,' said Nubia, echoing his thoughts.

'It's against the law to take a body off the cross,' explained Aristo. 'The point of such punishment is that nothing remain of the body and therefore of the victim's memory. That poor wretch's relatives probably took him down under cover of night, in order to give him a proper funeral.'

They were passing between the crosses now, close enough to read the signs scrawled in Greek with red paint. Above the grisly remains, a plank stated: RUNAWAY SLAVE.

The sign over the empty cross read: ATHEIST

'What does that mean?' asked Nubia.

'An atheist is someone who doesn't believe in the gods.' Aristo glanced at Jonathan. 'He was probably a Jew, or – more likely – a Christian.'

'But they believe in a god,' said Flavia.

'They don't believe in our gods,' said Aristo. 'I mean the Greek and Roman gods, and most importantly the imperial cult.'

'Is that a crime?' asked Nubia.

'It's considered subversive. Mind you, the Jews have been living here in Asia for centuries and the Romans allow them to worship according to their laws. Until recently the authorities included Christians in the same category. But recently many Jews argue that Christianity is not just a sect of Judaism, but a separate religion.' He looked at Jonathan. 'Your father told me that.'

Lupus shuddered. He could still see the dark stains of blood on the empty cross, where the nails had pierced the man's wrists and heels.

They entered Ephesus as the sun was sinking over the Aegean, making the water an expanse of molten bronze. The dome of the sky was very high and the sea breeze ruffled their hair and tunics. Flavia's limbs were aching and her stomach was upset, so they stopped at the first inn they found, a small hospitium inside the Magnesian

Gate, near a large nymphaeum on the southern side of the street. While Nubia made sure the horses were comfortably stalled and Aristo negotiated the price of a room with the innkeeper, Flavia went straight to the latrine. After some time she made her way back to the main part of the hospitium and found the boys in a cool, thick-walled room which gave onto a vine-shaded courtyard. There was a long low sleeping platform on one side of the room, with mattresses spread out on it. Flavia lay down on the mattress nearest the door; it was made of cloth and very firm, but more comfortable than the straw mattresses they had encountered so far.

She was just dozing off when Aristo's voice startled her awake. Nubia was beside him, her bath-set in her hand.

'I've paid a few local urchins a reward if they can tell me where Mindius is, and if Bato has arrested him. We should have an answer in an hour or so. In the meantime, I suggest we visit the public baths next door and have a nice soak before dinner. Until we find out where Mindius is, there's nothing we can do.'

An hour in the bathhouse had made Jonathan feel clean and relaxed. For the moment the voice was silent. Back at the hospitium, dinner was being served. Lupus was fast asleep in their room, but its door gave onto the cool evening courtyard so Jonathan was not worried about his friend sneaking out again. Nubia was tossing crumbs of bread to some friendly sparrows. Flavia was still subdued; she had barely touched the gustatio of cheese and pickled onions. A slave had lit the torches in their wall brackets, and they were just beginning the prima mensa – a barley gruel with chunks of unidentifiable meat – when the innkeeper's wife came into the court-yard. She was followed by two soldiers flanking a thin man with a pockmarked face.

She stood scowling at them with her hands on her hips. Then she pointed. 'That's them,' she said. 'That's the ones named on the notice in the Upper Agora. They're dressed as boys, but I think those two are girls.' She pointed at Flavia and Nubia, then swivelled her outstretched arm towards the bedroom where Lupus was sleeping. 'The youngest one is asleep in there. Now, where's my reward? Where's my four thousand drachmae?'

The market basilica of Ephesus was a magnificent structure of marble and granite, with an inlaid floor and lofty columns. But the cells at its back were dark and damp. Jonathan was already wheezing by the time the official ushered them into a small cell with an earth floor and a ceiling so low they had to crouch to enter. The jailer's flickering torch briefly showed a pile of dark rags in one corner of the cell, perhaps a former prisoner's bedding. Jonathan's nose told him another corner had been used as a latrine.

The heavy wooden door slammed shut behind them, plunging them into darkness.

Jonathan sank slowly to the beaten earth floor. He felt the damp, cold stone against his back and pressed his herb pouch to his nose.

'This is a disaster,' he muttered to himself.

'For once, you're right,' came Flavia's voice. Jonathan could tell she was trying not to cry. 'Things could hardly get any worse.'

'Will they crucify us?' whispered Nubia.

'No,' came Flavia's voice. 'I mean, I hope not.'

A thin rectangle of dark blue at the far end of the cell must have been a window letting in a little starlight. As Jonathan's eyes adjusted, he could dimly see Flavia and Nubia with their arms around each other. Lupus had curled up miserably in his woollen cloak, too exhausted even to grunt.

'How did the innkeeper's wife know who we were?' said Flavia. 'Nubia and I were dressed as boys.'

'Maybe the fact that you kept calling each other "Flavia" and "Nubia"?' wheezed Jonathan. 'We should have adopted pseudonyms.'

'What is soon oh dim?' asked Nubia in a small voice.

'Pseudonym,' sighed Flavia, 'is Greek for "false name", often one which will mislead people.'

'We could call Flavia "Placida",' said Jonathan sarcastically, 'because she's so meek and obedient.'

'Yes,' came Flavia's retort. 'And we could call you "Hilarius". That would fool everybody.'

'If you want to mislead people,' muttered Jonathan, 'why not call me "Sanus"? Because I think I'm going mad.'

'Why do you think you are going mad?' said Nubia softly.

For a long time Jonathan didn't answer. Then he said. 'Since we left Egypt, I've been hearing a voice in my head.'

'Is it your god?' asked Flavia.

'Definitely not. If anything, it's the opposite. It's evil.'

'You are hearing an evil voice?' asked Nubia. 'When no person is there?'

'Yes. I know it's inside my head but sometimes it's like someone talking to me.'

'Oh dear,' said Flavia. 'That's not good.'

'I know.'

'What is the voice saying?' asked Nubia.

'REJOICE!' came a deep raspy shout.

Flavia and Nubia screamed, Lupus grunted in alarm, and Jonathan cracked his head on the ceiling as he jumped up.

'Ow!' he cried, rubbing his head, and then: 'Who's there? Who are you?'

'I will say it again!' The voice came from the far corner of the cell: 'Rejoice!'

'Stay back or I'll hit you!' wheezed Jonathan. 'I'm a trained boxer.' His own voice sounded feeble and unconvincing.

'Who are you?' came Nubia's soft voice.

'My name is Cleopas,' rasped the voice. 'Silversmith and worker of gems. Let us sing hymns of praise to the Lord. Rejoice!'

'He's mad,' muttered Flavia.

'No. He's Jewish,' said Jonathan.

'I am,' came the raspy voice, and added: 'And I'm telling you to praise the Lord in all things.'

'What did you do?' said Nubia gently. 'What crime?'

'Nothing! I did nothing. Nothing but preach the good news.'

'A Christian!' cried Flavia.

'Yes, I follow The Way. But my rival, Thallus, is taking me to court tomorrow. He's a silversmith like me. He says the Christians put his father out of business several years ago and that now I'm trying to do the same thing.'

'Will they crucify you?' whispered Nubia.

'I hope not. I think he only wants my shop. But if they do execute me, at least I know where I'm going afterwards. And so I am rejoicing! And so should you.'

'What do *we* have to be thankful for?' came Flavia's grumpy voice.

The voice of Cleopas chuckled in the darkness. 'Surely there is something.'

Jonathan sighed. 'I suppose,' he said, 'we should be grateful that it's nice and cool in here. For the first time in a week I'm not pouring with sweat.'

'We could be thankful that Aristo gave us our cloaks,' said Flavia. 'We can use them to lie on.'

'And that they did not arrest Aristo,' came Nubia's voice.

'Also,' added Flavia. 'maybe now we'll find out why we're wanted.'

'Unless they kill us first,' muttered Jonathan.

'I don't think they can just kill us,' said Flavia. 'There are rules. Laws and rules.'

'They tried to kill Lupus when we were in Middle Egypt,' Jonathan pointed out.

'That was Taurus's slave. He wanted us out of the way because we were the only ones who knew his master had kept the gem for himself. And he probably bribed the governor's official to help him. But that was in Egypt. I don't think anyone in Asia would want to kill us. I *hope* they won't.'

'Who has summoned you to court?' came Cleopas's gravelly voice.

'Titus,' said Jonathan. 'The Emperor Titus.'

'Oh,' said Cleopas. And after a pause: 'I think you should stop rejoicing and start praying.'

In his vision he sees the battle in the constellation of the Maiden, the star sign of Virgo. Lucifer, the Morning Star, is struggling with a smaller star. The smaller star is golden and has the ears of a satyr. He represents Midas. Midas with the golden touch. Midas, the proud king humbled by the gods. Lucifer is beautiful, an angel dressed in robes of silver and with a sword of rubies. But he is fallen, and Midas is redeemed. Midas must win, or all is lost. Goat-eared Midas is the Key to this battle.

SCROLL XIII

'Up you get!' said a man's voice in Greek. 'They're taking you away.'

For a moment Flavia couldn't remember where she was.

Then she saw the dim stone walls of the cell, and her three friends curled up beside her on an earthen floor. The thin rectangle of pale yellow sky in the window slit told her it was dawn.

'Come on!' growled the jailer. He was crouching in the low doorway, glaring in at them. 'I said get up. This isn't a hospitium!'

Flavia bumped her head on the stone roof of the cell as she stood. She groaned and rubbed the sore spot. Beside her Jonathan and Nubia were stirring. Lupus was still asleep. And in the corner a man of about thirty was peering at her with interest. He had a thin face and bright black eyes.

'I am Cleopas,' he said. 'And I'm guessing you are Flavia. Or should I call you Placida?'

Flavia nodded at him and gave him a queasy smile. She felt sick with apprehension.

'Rejoice!' whispered Cleopas, as Flavia crouched to go through the doorway. 'May the Lord bless you and make his face to shine upon you. Rejoice in all things.'

She could hear him praying as she followed the jailer up the stairs.

The torches were burning in the courtyard, but dawn's light showed Marcus Artorius Bato flanked by two soldiers. His expression was cold.

'You!' cried Flavia, her fear turning to anger. 'You traitor!'

Bato ignored her. 'Here is my imperial mandate,' he said to the jailer.

'Can't read,' said the jailer.

'Well, you recognise that seal, don't you?'

The jailer nodded. 'Maybe I should wait until my—'

'No need to wait,' interrupted Bato. 'I'll keep the four of them under house arrest until I can take them back to Italia. Here's enough gold to cover the reward.' He handed a small leather bag to the jailer. Bato lowered his voice. 'And this is for you and your superior.' Flavia heard the soft chink of silver.

The jailer hesitated, then nodded and moved back towards the basilica.

'Take them,' said Bato to his soldiers. He turned abruptly to lead the way out of the courtyard.

One of the soldiers roughly pushed Flavia forward, and she felt fresh tears welling up. Bato had come to Asia to help her father find kidnapped children. How could he betray her and the others?

They emerged into the early morning and walked past an imposing, colonnaded building. Once past it, they turned right down one of the broad paved streets. The citizens of Ephesus were already out and about; workers in sleeveless tunics, merchants in coloured cloaks, magistrates and officials in Roman-style togas. A few gave them curious looks, but most hurried by without a second glance.

They passed the theatre on their left, then a busy market on their right, as well as numerous fountains and shrines. The sky was getting lighter every moment. It had been cold in the cell but it was warm and bright out here and the swallows were already swooping low over the streets.

The four friends followed Bato in single-file, with one soldier walking before them and one behind. No one had put manacles on them, and for a moment Flavia was tempted to run away. She glanced over her shoulder at her friends; would they be willing make a dash for freedom? Jonathan was breathing from his herb pouch, Nubia was fighting to hold tears back and Lupus stared blearily ahead. The swarthy soldier taking up the rear caught her gaze and narrowed his fierce blue eyes in warning.

Flavia sighed and turned away from his glare. 'Oh Castor and Pollux,' she whispered. 'Please help us!'

Now they turned left onto a wide paved street which angled up the slope of a north-facing hill. A right turn led them up among residential houses built into the terraced slope. Although most of the houses presented unimposing faces to the street, Flavia could tell this was a wealthy part of town: violets in upstairs flower-boxes, clean pavements and no smelly or noisy industry nearby.

Finally, Bato stopped in front of wooden double doors shaded by a porch and flanked by two ionic columns. Before he could knock, the doors swung open and Aristo appeared in the vestibule, a look of extreme worry on his face.

'Aristo!' cried Flavia. 'Bato betrayed us. He had us arrested! Do something!'

'Calm down, Flavia,' said Aristo. 'Bato hasn't arrested you. I managed to track him down last night and tell him what happened. He's only pretending to keep you under house arrest so nobody else can claim you. He's put his career at risk for you.'

Bato turned and lifted one eyebrow in a sardonic expression. 'After you, Flavia Gemina,' he said, standing aside to let her go first.

Flavia felt her cheeks flushing and she rushed past him into the safety of the house and Aristo's reassuring embrace.

'I'm so sorry you had to spend the night in the cells.' Aristo gave her a quick squeeze and released her. 'I felt so powerless when they took you away ... Are you all right?' He was looking at Nubia.

'Yes,' said Nubia. 'We are unharmed.'

'At least you gave us the cloaks,' said Flavia. 'Thank you.' She took a deep breath and turned to Bato. 'And thank you for rescuing us, Marcus Artorius Bato. I'm sorry I called you a traitor.'

He gave a little bow and she saw a half-smile play about his lips.

'Where are we?' asked Jonathan, looking around. For the first time, Flavia noticed the richness and size of the atrium. It was two stories tall, with rooms giving onto it and a colonnaded balcony running around the upper storey. The Egyptian blue panels on the frescoed walls glowed like lapis lazuli in the brightening light.

'Yes,' she breathed. 'Where is this?'

'This,' said Bato, 'is the Villa Vinea, the Ephesian townhouse of Mindius Faustus.' He gestured towards the now-familiar portrait of the serious-looking man with dark hair and eyes.

Flavia clapped her hands. 'Have you arrested him? Did you find Popo?'

'I'm afraid not. My men and I have been here since yesterday, lying in wait for him. We've occupied this villa and we've been watching both town gates and the harbour, too, just in case. But so far there is no sign of him. Or the baby.' Bato pulled aside an embroidered curtain and gestured towards a table already set with six places. At its centre was a platter of pomegranates, split to reveal the ruby-red seeds inside. 'Let's sit and have some breakfast. Afterwards I'll show you the rest of the house. And the children.'

'The children?' said Flavia. There was a silver bowl of rose-scented water on a small citrus-wood table just inside the doorway. She washed her hands and dried them on the towel provided, then went to sit beside Nubia, who had chosen a chair facing the atrium. As Flavia sat down, she looked up and saw Bato's two soldiers pass through. The fierce-looking one gave her a wink.

Aristo and Bato each took an end of the table and the boys sat opposite Flavia and Nubia. For a moment they all ate silently, staining their fingers pink as they picked the red pomegranate seeds from their husks.

Presently a fat woman in a long beige tunic brought in a tray with six bowls of porridge and a jug of apple tea.

'Daphne here is the cook,' said Bato. 'She's the only one of the slaves who didn't run away.'

The woman smiled at them and then went out of the room.

Flavia watched Lupus spoon porridge into his beaker of apple tea. He stirred it, then carefully tipped it down his throat. He was bleary-eyed and the scratches on his cheeks were still red.

Bato took a jar from the table and sniffed its contents. 'You know you're in the Roman Empire,' he said, 'when you can find garum on the table.' He poured some of the thin brown liquid into his porridge and without looking up he said, 'Now, would you mind telling me why there is a warrant for your arrest?'

Flavia looked at Jonathan, and he said: 'We went on a mission for the emperor last March.'

'Ah ha,' said Bato, stirring the fish sauce into his porridge. 'I thought as much. Titus wrote me a letter last winter asking me about your suitability for a mission.' Bato drizzled some thyme-scented honey onto his porridge. 'May I ask what the mission was?'

'He didn't tell you?' asked Jonathan.

'No,' Bato said with a tight smile. 'He didn't deem it relevant.'

'He wanted us to find a gem called "Nero's Eye",' said Flavia, 'and bring it back to him. He gave us each an imperial pass and some money.'

'What went wrong?'

'Nothing!' said Flavia. 'We found the gem in Volubilis. But Titus's agent took the gem.'

'Titus's agent? What was his name?'

'Taurus,' said Jonathan.

Bato froze with the spoon halfway to his mouth. 'Statilius Taurus?'

'Yes.'

'Do you still have the letter? Or the passes?' Bato carefully placed his spoon back in the bowl. 'Or any other proof that Titus sent you on this mission?'

Flavia shook her head. 'Nubia and Lupus lost their passes in the shipwreck and some officials in Alexandria confiscated my pass, and Jonathan's.'

'Anyway,' said Jonathan. 'In the letter Titus said that if we were caught, he would disavow all knowledge of our actions.'

Flavia frowned. 'No, Jonathan, that wasn't in the letter. Taurus told us that when we were at his house in Sabratha. What?' she cried, seeing the expression on Bato's face.

'Taurus arrived in Rome a few months ago,' said Bato. 'And within days of his arrival he took up residence in an opulent townhouse. Rumour says it was a gift of Domitian.'

'Domitian?' said Flavia sharply. 'Not Titus?'

'Domitian,' said Bato.

'You might not know this,' said Aristo to the four friends, 'But in the last half year Titus's headaches have been getting worse and worse.'

Bato nodded. 'Rumour says he spends whole days in a darkened room. He's virtually given over the running of the Empire to his brother.'

'So if Domitian gave Taurus a townhouse . . .' began Flavia.

'A very opulent townhouse,' interrupted Bato, 'on the Palatine Hill.'

'Then it must have been a reward for something big.'

'Something like "Nero's Eye"?' said Jonathan.

'Great Juno's peacock!' exclaimed Flavia, her eyes blazing. 'Taurus didn't want the gem for himself! He was working for Domitian!'

SCROLL XIV

'Domitian hired Taurus to get the gem for himself!' cried Flavia. 'Taurus let us do all the work and then took it from us.'

Bato nodded. 'So it would seem.'

'And Titus thinks we betrayed him!' continued Flavia. 'And so he put out the decree for our arrest.'

'Or,' said Bato. 'Domitian put out the warrant in his brother's name. He wants you arrested – or possibly worse – so you can't tell Titus that you succeeded in your mission but were betrayed by Taurus—'

'—who was working for Domitian!' said Flavia.

'And apart from Taurus and his henchman Pullo,' said Jonathan, 'we're the only ones who know about it. No wonder Domitian wants us dead.'

Flavia put down her spoon. She had suddenly lost her appetite. 'We're doomed,' she said.

'Maybe not,' said Bato. 'Not if I can convince the authorities that you're dead.'

Jonathan gave a bitter laugh. 'We tried that before,' he said. 'In Egypt. It didn't work.'

'I'll send a courier to Rome,' said Bato. 'I'll make sure it reaches the Imperial Palace. But the four of you must lay low. Change your names, your appearances.' Flavia saw him look at Nubia and shake his head. She was gazing back at him with her beautiful golden eyes. 'Or at least stay inside as much as possible,' he added. 'Does anybody in Ephesus know your name?' he asked. 'Apart from the landlady last night?'

The friends looked at each other, then Flavia shook her head. 'I don't think so.'

'Prisoner in our cell last night,' said Nubia.

'There was someone with you?' asked Aristo.

'Yes,' said Jonathan. 'A Jew named Cleopas.'

'What was he arrested for?' asked Bato. 'I can try to deal with him. Perhaps if I get him off he'll stay quiet.'

'He was arrested for preaching the good news,' said Jonathan. 'He's a Christian.'

Bato snorted. 'Christians!' he said. 'Asia is crawling with them. Flaccus and I were discussing them only last week.'

At the mention of Flaccus, Flavia looked up eagerly. 'What did Flaccus say?'

'He said this Jewish sect called Christianity is a threat to the Roman way of life.'

'Why?' asked Jonathan.

Bato shrugged. 'According to Flaccus, they're subversive. They refuse to observe the imperial cult and in so doing, they scorn Roman rule. Also, they're irrational. They believe without reasoning out their argument. Flaccus says their leader was a magician who healed the sick and freed those possessed by demons. His followers claim to do the same things. These Christians also preach a resurrection of the dead. Imagine believing that a dead person could come alive again!' He took a sip of apple tea and looked around at them all. 'I think the four of you should stay here. I can make good use of you,' he said. 'We've found fifty more captured children in this villa.'

'Fifty!' cried Nubia.

'Yes. I presume you saw how Flaccus and Prudentilla processed the ones at Halicarnassus? Could you four do the same thing?'

'Of course,' said Flavia. 'We can do it as well as they can.'

'They were using dolls,' said Nubia.

'Dolls?' said Bato.

Jonathan stared into his empty porridge bowl. 'It helps the frightened ones to talk about painful things.'

'Then you know how it's done. Good. There are some very wretched children here.'

'Another carpet factory?' said Flavia.

'Yes,' said Bato. 'But he also had a dozen children installed in more comfortable quarters. He was grooming them for something else.'

Flavia saw Bato give Aristo a meaningful glance.

'But what about baby Popo?' she asked. 'Aren't we going to try to rescue him?'

'Until we know where Mindius is,' said Bato, 'we have no way of knowing where the baby is. My men will let me know as soon as he sets foot inside this town. Let me look for Mindius; you help the children.' He drained his beaker and plunked it down emphatically. 'No point delaying,' he said. 'I'll take you to them now.'

Nubia thought Mindius's Ephesian villa was one of the most beautiful houses she had ever seen. It had four inner courtyards, twenty-six bedrooms, three dining rooms, a tablinum, a library and even a baths complex with latrines. Some of the upper bedrooms on the north side had balconies overlooking Ephesus. There was also a big high-vaulted kitchen with two long cooking hearths and a stone sink containing water piped from one of the aqueducts.

The most impressive courtyard was a canal garden, built into the southern slope of the hill. At the far end of the garden a waterfall splashed out of a mosaic and shell fountain set between two platforms. Mats and cushions could be laid on these platforms to make couches for an outdoor triclinium. The waterfall fed into a shallow canal running lengthwise through the middle of the garden. Lush grape arbours gave shade on either side of this canal, along with peach and carob trees.

'That must be why they call it the Villa Vinea,' said Flavia, looking up at the grapes hanging from the vines.

Nubia nodded, then smiled as Lupus jumped up onto a marble bench and then stood on tiptoes in order to pick a grape.

Mindius's villa also had a vegetable garden courtyard with blue-veined marble pillars for the colonnade. Painted marble oscilla hung between these columns. These revolving discs had pictures of medusas and satyrs on them, to scare away birds. A massive fig tree shaded a third courtyard with a circular mosaic of Orpheus surrounded by animals. The fourth courtyard boasted a swimming pool with four lofty date palms: one at each corner. As they came into the palm tree courtyard, Lupus pulled off his tunic and leapt into the pool, wearing only his loincloth. He landed like a boulder from a ballista, splashing them all.

The friends and Aristo laughed, and even Bato gave a half-smile as he brushed drops of water from his toga.

'The Villa Vinea reminds me of Cordius's villa,' murmured Flavia.

Nubia nodded her agreement. Cordius was the patron of Flavia's father. He had an opulent townhouse in Ostia which occupied an entire insula. At the thought of Ostia, a sudden wave of homesickness washed over her. Even though she had grown up in the desert, she had grown to love Roman houses, with their secret inner gardens, colonnaded walkways and splashing fountains. The thought of Ostia also made her think of her beloved dog Nipur who must be wondering why she did not return to him. Nubia swallowed hard and blinked back tears.

Bato showed them the villa's small but luxurious bath complex. There were changing rooms, a frigidarium and a small domed caldarium of apricot-coloured marble. Next to the bath complex was a marble six-seater latrine with a trough of running water piped from the baths complex.

In the tablinum, a luxurious study off the canal garden, everything gleamed, for the pens, inkwells and even the bronze oil-lamps were gilded.

'It's like the palace of Midas,' said Flavia, picking up a scroll with gilded bosses at each end. It was a scroll of Herodotus, written in Greek.

'Who is Midas?' asked Nubia, examining a gilded quill pen in wonder.

'He was a king of Phrygia,' said Flavia. 'One of the gods said he could have any wish he wanted. So Midas wished that everything he touched might turn to gold.'

Lupus came in, dripping wet and leaving damp foot-prints. He had heard Flavia's last words and pretended to be Midas, touching various objects and jumping back in delight as they turned to gold.

'To become rich!' said Nubia.

'At first he thought so,' said Flavia. 'But then it all went wrong.'

Lupus picked up an apple from a bowl on the desk and pretended to crack a tooth in trying to bite it.

'Oh!' said Nubia.

'That's right,' said Flavia. 'Food turned to gold and wine turned to liquid gold.'

'And there were other problems,' grinned Jonathan, as Lupus approached with his finger extended. As soon as Lupus touched him, Jonathan obligingly pretended to become a statue.

'Alas!' cried Nubia.

'Exactly,' said Flavia. 'When Midas's only daughter ran into his arms, she was turned to gold, too. Luckily the gods took pity and reversed his wish.' Flavia put the scroll back in a niche. 'Later, Midas was cursed with hairy pointed satyr ears,' she said.

'Served him right,' said Jonathan, unfreezing. He looked around. 'What does Mindius need such a big house for, anyway? He's not even married.'

'Not that we know of,' said Bato. 'My guess is he entertains potential buyers here.'

Next Bato took them to the carpet factory. Constructed like the one in Halicarnassus, it was little more than a wooden shack, hot and dim.

'The weavers are all boys,' said Bato, leading them out of the stuffy building to the stables next door. 'Last night we unchained them and fed them. They sleep in here.'

After the stench of the carpet factory, the scent of the stables was glorious and Nubia exclaimed with joy to see her beloved Tarquin and the other horses they had ridden from Halicarnassus. There were three other horses here, too, and she knew these must belong to Bato and his soldiers. As Nubia ran forward to greet Tarquin she saw inside some of the stalls and gasped. She had presumed the stalls to be empty, but they were full of boys, fast asleep on the hay. Each horse had its own stall, but the boys had to share, three or four together. Nubia counted twenty of them, aged four to nine.

'Poor lads are exhausted,' Bato explained. 'We arrived at dusk the night before last and they were still at work. The overseer and most of the other villa staff ran off when we got here. But Daphne the cook stayed behind and offered to help us. She belongs to some local guild. She told the leader of the guild and he's organised a delivery of clean tunics for the boys.'

'What is a guild?' asked Nubia over her shoulder; she was stroking Tarquin's nose. 'I always forget that word.'

'A guild is just a group of people who share a philo-sophy,' said Bato. 'They often work in the same trade and worship a particular god or goddess. Most of the guilds in this city revere Artemis.' He turned to Jonathan. 'The tunics should be here in the next hour or two. In the meantime, will you and Lupus take the boys to the baths? Spend all morning. Get them to leave their old lice-infested clothes on the ground outside, not in the changing room. I'll get one of my men to burn them. When the boys are clean we can move them into the bedrooms.'

'Have they eaten?' asked Flavia.

Bato nodded. 'Last night Daphne the cook made them a veritable feast. That's why they're all still sleep-ing.' He looked at Aristo. 'I hope you'll stay and help me. There's plenty of room and until those imperial notices come down it's probably the safest place for the children.'

'Of course we'll stay,' said Aristo. 'We are very grateful.'

While Jonathan and Lupus took the boys to the baths, Bato showed Flavia, Nubia and Aristo the slave quarters at the back of the main building. Compared to the stables, the small individual cubicles were luxurious, with rush sleeping mats and cool, plaster-lined walls.

'This is where the chosen few slept,' said Bato grimly. 'They're waiting in the fig tree courtyard. Aristo, you can speak to the two boys.' He turned to Nubia and Flavia. 'Will you speak to the girls?'

Nubia nodded and Flavia said: 'Of course.'

Bato took them back to the Orpheus courtyard with its cedarwood benches beneath the shade of an ancient fig tree. It reminded Nubia of Flavia's garden in Ostia and she felt another sudden pang of bittersweet home-sickness.

The twelve favoured children ranged in age from six to thirteen, the eldest being twin Persian boys called Darius and Cyrus. These children were not thin and grubby like the carpet-weavers; they were clean, plump and well groomed. And they were all strikingly beautiful.

All twelve children spoke Greek, but only one seemed to understand Latin, a lovely looking girl of about eleven with curly brown hair and eyes the colour of sapphires. Although she obviously understood what they were saying, she would not tell them her name.

Nubia asked Aristo if he had brought her travelling basket. He nodded and disappeared in the direction of the atrium. A few moments later he was back, with her basket and Flavia's. Nubia reached into her basket and pulled out the two dolls which Prudentilla had given her. She handed the blue-haired one to the girl who understood Latin.

'My name is Nubia,' Nubia made her doll say. 'I am from Nubia but also from Italia. What is your name?'

The blue-haired doll was silent.

'Where are you from?' asked Nubia gently, still using her mustard-haired doll. 'Can you nod or shake your head?'

The girl with sapphire-coloured eyes made her doll nod.

'Are you from here?'

The girl's doll shook its head.

'Egypt? Greece? Italia?'

The girl made her doll nod its head.

'You're from Italia? So are we. We are from Ostia, the port of Rome.'

'So am I,' the girl made her doll say. 'I'm from Ostia, too.'

'You're from Ostia?' cried Flavia. 'What's your name?'

The girl lowered her eyes.

'What is your name?' Nubia made her doll ask the girl's doll.

'Sapphira,' said the girl's doll.

'Oh!' cried Flavia. 'When I was younger there were rumours that a girl called Sapphira was kidnapped by Venalicius and sold to a Syrian merchant!'

Sapphira was silent, her eyes still downcast.

Nubia moved her doll forward. 'I was captured by Venalicius, too. Some bad men killed my family and brought me to him.' She made her doll speak softly.

Flavia took the hint and addressed Nubia's doll rather than Sapphira's. 'What did Venalicius do to you?'

'He put a chain around my neck,' Nubia made her doll say. 'He sold me naked. I felt very ashamed.' Nubia turned her doll to face Sapphira's: 'Did Venalicius take you, too?'

'Yes,' said Sapphira's doll in an almost inaudible voice. 'Venalicius brought some of us to Rhodes, to a dwarf. He sent me to Halicarnassus, to a man called Mindius. He brought me here. I hate him.'

'Did he hurt you?' Nubia's doll asked Sapphira's doll.

Sapphira's doll was silent.

'The other children weave carpets,' said Nubia's doll after a moment. 'What do you do?'

'They train us to sing and dance,' said Sapphira's doll. 'They teach us to serve at dinner and to give massage in the baths.'

'Do you like doing that?'

Sapphira gripped her doll tightly and shook her head. Then she began to grind its wooden face against the marble bench. 'No,' she whispered, erasing the doll's painted features. 'I hate it.'

SCROLL XV

In addition to Sapphira, there were nine other little girls in the special slave quarters of the Villa Vinea. Nubia's Greek was now almost as good as her Latin and she was able to comfort them, too. Soon she had them all making dolls with scraps of wool from the carpet factory and bits of one of Mindius's old tunics. She had also found three kittens in a corner of the large kitchen.

The girls were happy sitting in the shade of the fig tree with Nubia and their dolls and the kittens, so Flavia went to find the boys. She was not as good as Nubia at comforting the little girls and she wanted to be doing something useful, not just sitting in the shade and playing dolls. Every moment her baby cousin might be further away.

Flavia found the carpet-weaving boys in the canal garden, sitting in the dappled shade beneath the grape arbours. They were clean and bathed and fed. One of Bato's soldiers had shaved their lice-infested hair. A few of the older ones were wearing Mindius's tunics but most were wearing the new tunics donated by someone called Aquila the Tentmaker. But even clean and wearing new tunics, the boys were a heartbreaking sight. Many of them had swollen red eyes and scarred fingertips. Some of the older boys were hunched over, like little old men. Many had hacking coughs. Jonathan had told her that almost all of them had weals on their backs from being beaten with rods.

Flavia stood in the shadow of a column and watched them.

Jonathan sat on the right-hand platform of the summer triclinium by the mosaic wall-fountain. He was holding a gilded abacus from Mindius's tablinum and showing a few of the older boys how to do simple calculations. Three sat on the platform opposite him and two on the soft grass. All five were watching him with shining eyes. A loud burst of laughter came from another corner of the garden, and Flavia turned to see Lupus sitting in the shade of a carob tree with the rest of the boys. They were throwing dice and gambling for carob pods.

Aristo emerged from Mindius's tablinum, his wax tablet in hand. All morning he had been going back and forth between the boys' courtyard and the girls', writing down as many details as he could about the children. Soon Bato would post some details of the children in the forum, holding back one or two vital facts, enough to make sure the people who claimed the children were really their families.

Already, three of the boys had been claimed by fathers saying they had been too afraid of Mindius to rescue their sons.

'Probably sold their boys to him in the first place,' Bato had grumbled. 'And they'll probably work them as hard on their farm or in the fullers'.'

'At least they're with their families,' Aristo had replied.

Seeing Aristo come out of the tablinum gave Flavia an idea. Maybe she could find some clues in Mindius's study. She moved along the shaded colonnade towards the wide doorway.

But when she went in, she saw Bato sitting at the gilded table, going through papyrus sheets which looked like accounts. He looked up at her and gave a tired smile.

'How goes it with the little girls?' he asked.

'Nubia's with them. They love her. She's so gentle and kind. The carpet-boys love Lupus. Some of the older ones even like moody old Jonathan.'

'Yes,' said Bato. 'You're all doing—'

'Sir!' said a man's breathless voice from the doorway. 'We've just had a sighting ... of Mindius. He's been travelling ... with that prophet ... Tychicus ... for the past few days.' It was the soldier with the fierce blue eyes.

'What?' cried Bato.

'A cobbler ... from the harbour agora ... swears it was him.'

Bato cursed. 'He must have known he was being followed and decided to hide among the crowds. A clever move.'

'Great Juno's peacock!' exclaimed Flavia. 'We rode right past him! If we'd stopped we might have caught him!'

Bato's chair scraped on the marble floor as he stood up. 'Is Mindius still travelling with the prophet?'

'No, sir!' The soldier had caught his breath. 'My informant said he was on his way to a Hierapolis.'

'Hierapolis?'

'Town about a hundred miles west of here, sir. Hot springs and a temple to Diana.'

'Was he alone?' Flavia asked the soldier. 'Was Mindius alone?'

'No.' The soldier's blue eyes flickered sideways to Flavia, but he addressed his reply to Bato. 'Had a woman with him. And a baby, too.'

'And a huge bodyguard?' asked Bato, taking his toga from the chair.

'No sir, according to my source it was just the three of them. Mindius, the woman and the baby. On two horses. Making their way to Hierapolis.'

Bato looked at Flavia. 'I should have told you before, but I didn't want to worry you,' he said.

'What?' said Flavia. 'What should you have told us?'

'Before I left Halicarnassus, I asked that dwarf Magnus why Mindius had taken your baby cousin.'

'And?' said Flavia.

Bato looked down at the floor and his jaw clenched. 'He said that Mindius intended to offer the child as a sacrifice to the gods.'

'Nubia!' cried Flavia, running into the Orpheus courtyard. 'Mindius has taken Miriam's baby to a place called Hierapolis! He's going to sacrifice Popo to the gods! We have to go!'

Nubia was sitting with some little girls on a cedarwood bench in the shade of the fig tree. She looked up at Flavia, her golden eyes wide. 'I did not think Romans sacrifice babies.'

'We don't! But Mindius is evil!'

As Nubia rose from the bench, one of the little girls – Euodia – wrapped her arms around Nubia's legs. 'Don't go, Nubia!' the little girl cried in Greek. 'Don't go away.'

Nubia looked down at the girls, then back up at Flavia.

'Hurry, Nubia!' cried Flavia. 'Bato says we can come with him, but only if we leave right now. I told him we'd follow him anyway, so he might as well take us. The boys are coming, too,' she added.

Now two of the other girls were hugging Nubia's legs. The youngest sat with her thumb in her mouth looking up at Nubia with liquid dark eyes. Nubia glanced down at Sapphira. A few moments ago she had been smiling and petting one of the kittens. Now her face was an expressionless mask.

'I will stay here with Sapphira and the girls,' said Nubia. 'You go.'

'Are you sure?' said Flavia. 'You're the best rider of us all.'

'I am sure. I will stay here. They need someone to care for them until they are reunited with their families.'

'But, Nubia, we're a team.'

'I am still in your team,' said Nubia. 'But the girls need me. I will wait for you here, with them.'

She sat back down on the cedarwood bench. The little girls clutched Nubia and glared up defiantly at Flavia, as if she were the enemy.

Flavia swallowed hard and quickly turned away, before Nubia could see her tears.

'What's happening, Flavia?' Aristo emerged from between two columns, followed by some of the carpet-boys. 'Where are you going?'

'Lupus and Jonathan and I are going with Bato to save Popo from Mindius,' said Flavia. 'And there's nothing you can do or say to stop us.'

Aristo sighed and closed his eyes and shook his head. Then he looked at Nubia. 'You, too?'

'No,' said Flavia, in a low voice. 'She's staying here with the children. Aristo, maybe you should stay with her.'

'What?'

'Bato said he's trying to find someone reliable to help Daphne look after the children,' said Flavia. 'But until he does, the children trust Nubia. Will you stay and protect her?'

'I'm supposed to be protecting all of you.' He looked at Flavia. 'And it's your father who employs me. By all the gods, you've just got out of prison!'

'I'll dress as a boy,' said Flavia. 'And Bato and two of his best men will be with us. If anyone asks they can say we're in custody. Aristo, I *have* to save Popo. Please stay with Nubia and the children?'

Aristo did not reply, but he nodded.

'May the gods protect you,' whispered Flavia, fighting back fresh tears.

'And you,' said Aristo. He put a hand on her shoulder. 'I can't believe I'm saying this, but: act like a boy!'

Flavia nodded and tried to smile bravely. 'Just call me Placidus.'

From her mat Nubia called. 'Bring baby Popo back here and we will look after him.'

'Yes!' cried two of the little girls after her. 'Bring baby Popo.'

Before she went out of the courtyard, Flavia stopped and looked back. Aristo had gone to sit beside Nubia in the deep cool shade of the fig tree. With the boys and girls gathered around them, they looked like a family.

The Magnesian Gate had three arches: the first for pedestrian traffic, the second for riders and pack animals and the third for carts and carrucas. But a crowd had gathered around a pair of arguing women and the pedestrians had spilled over into the passage provided for riders and pack animals. There were so many people that Lupus's mare could barely move forward. Lupus reined her in and made a reassuring grunt. She stood patiently. She might be frightened of goats in the night, but she was obviously used to jostling crowds. From his vantage point, Lupus could see the two women causing the blockage.

'It's not him,' one of the women was saying.

'Yes, it is,' said the other; she wore a dark blue head-scarf. 'It's Erastus what begs in the Harbour Agora.'

'Must be someone who looks just like him,' said the first woman. 'Couldn't be Erastus. He's been blind from birth.'

'And now he's not. Look! It's him all right.'

The crowd shuffled and stirred, and now Lupus could see the women were arguing about a man. He had the typical dark hair and heavy eyebrows of a Phrygian, but his eyes were the eyes of an infant: a pure and startling blue in his tanned and weathered face.

'There are towers either side,' he said, gazing up at the Magnesian Gate with his new eyes. 'I never knew the gate had towers. And are those stone animals lions? Or panthers?'

'They're lions, of course,' laughed a blond youth. 'Haven't you ever seen a lion before?'

'Course he hasn't!' shouted the woman with the blue headscarf. 'I told you: he's been blind all his life. Until now, that is.'

'Is that true?' asked the blond.

The man looked at him with eyes full of delight. 'Yes,' he said. 'I am Erastus who was blind from birth. My parents will tell you. They live here in Ephesus.'

'Who healed you?' called the first woman.

'Tell us his name!' shouted an old man.

'Where is he?' said another.

'His name is Tychicus,' said Erastus. 'He used to travel with Paul of Tarsus. He's baptising in the Cayster River, up past the Temple of Artemis. It was when I came up out of the water that I could see!'

Lupus suddenly remembered what he was supposed to be doing. He looked around for Flavia and Jonathan. Flavia was following Bato and his two men, their horses like ships in a sea of faces. They were taking the road east, towards Magnesia and beyond.

But Jonathan had ridden his dun-coloured mare up beside Lupus.

'Go on, Lupus,' said Jonathan softly. 'I know you want to. You'll never know if you don't try. We should have stopped before, outside Heracleia. If we had, we might have found Popo and you might have been healed.'

Lupus pointed at Jonathan and then at himself, then raised his eyebrows.

'I can't come with you,' said Jonathan. 'I have to save Popo. But you should go and find the prophet who heals.'

Lupus looked at his friend for a long moment. Some deep sadness clouded Jonathan's eyes.

'Go!' whispered Jonathan. He whispered a prayer of protection in Hebrew, then turned away and urged Tiberina after Flavia, Bato and the two soldiers.

Lupus sat watching him go. His little bay mare stood calmly as a sea of people swirled around her. Something made Lupus look down, and he found himself gazing into the joyful new eyes of the former blind man.

The man smiled up at Lupus and for a heartbeat their gazes locked. Then Erastus was gone, pushed along by the people. When the crowd had swept him through the pedestrian arch of the town gate and out of sight, Lupus turned his mount north and started on the sacred way, towards where the prophet Tychicus was baptising believers and healing the sick.

SCROLL XVI

Lupus found Tychicus north of the city on the lush banks of the River Cayster, which some people called the Little Maeander. The prophet was not baptising or healing. He was speaking to the crowd.

Lupus rode close enough to hear what he was saying.

'Many of you are Jews,' cried Tychicus. 'You know the story of The Binding. How God told Abraham to sacrifice his son Isaac. The rabbis teach that Isaac was thirty years old when his father took him up Mount Moriah. Isaac was a man in the prime of life. Abraham over a hundred. And yet Isaac allowed his father Abraham to bind him. He was prepared to die. In the same way, God's own son went willingly to the cross. But no ram was supplied at the last moment, for Jesus himself was the lamb of God. He is your messiah. The anointed one.'

'You mean your god sacrificed his own son?' cried a woman. 'Instead of a sheep or a bull?'

'Yes!' cried Tychicus. 'And his death was more terrible than the most terrible thing you can imagine. But it had to be. Jesus was the sacrifice for all the bad things anyone would do ever again.'

'So it will save me a lot of money if I convert,' joked

a man in a pale-blue tunic. 'I'll never have to buy an animal for the sacrifice again!'

Some people laughed but Tychicus pointed at him and shouted, 'Exactly! No more animal sacrifice. Imagine it! A world without altars, a world without the daily slaughter of innocent creatures, a world without the smell of burnt flesh rising up into the heavens.'

'But it was cruel of God to kill his own son,' said the woman.

'Do you have children?' said Tychicus. 'Do you not suffer when they feel pain? So it was with God. He suffered, too.'

'Then why did he do it?' shouted another woman. 'If it caused him so much pain.'

'He did it for us,' said Tychicus. 'Because we are his children, too, and he loves us. He sacrificed his son once and for all people. And then he rewarded his son by bringing him back to life. Life eternal, and not in a body which grows old and decays, like this.' Tychicus thumped his chest with the hand that held the staff. 'A new body, resembling the old, but better and more real than before. So real that walls were like vapour and doors like dust in comparison. The resurrected Jesus could pass right through them.'

He spread his arms and looked around at the people.

'Imagine. A body which will live forever, whole and healthy, without disease or pain. And those of us who believe in him will share in this resurrection, so that one day we, too, will have these resurrection bodies.' Here he looked round at the crowd. 'But to share in his resurrection we must die to ourselves and be born from above.'

'What does that mean?' called a man's deep voice.

'How can a person be born from above?' a woman cried.

The joker in the blue tunic shouted out. 'I can't crawl back into my mother's womb.'

But others said: 'Quiet! Let him speak.'

Lupus nudged the mare closer, under the shade of a cypress tree.

'To be born from above,' cried Tychicus, 'is very easy. All you need to do is repent of your sins, accept Jesus as your lord, agree to follow his Way, and be baptised.'

'I already have a master!' shouted a man.

'What do you mean by sin?' cried a woman.

'What do you mean by way?' asked someone else.

'When you say yes to him, he will give you understanding,' said Tychicus. 'But don't leave it too late. The resurrected Lord is returning very soon. There is not much time left!'

Tychicus was already striding down through the crowd to the river. He waded out into the glittering water and when it had reached his waist he turned and waited for the people to come.

'Where's Lupus?' said Flavia to Jonathan.

It was mid afternoon and the road was passing through barley fields, white in the ferocious heat and brightness. She had reined in Herodotus and was waiting for Jonathan on his dun mare. Despite her wide-brimmed straw hat, her face felt sunburnt and sweat trickled down the back of her neck.

'Lupus left us at the Magnesian Gate,' said Jonathan. 'Didn't you notice?'

'I've been trying to keep up with them,' said Flavia, nodding towards the three riders on the road ahead. She urged Herodotus into motion again, so that she and Jonathan rode side by side. 'I wish Bato would slow down a little,' she said.

'You told him you'd be able to keep up.'

'I know. But they haven't taken a single break in the past two hours.'

'Exactly. We've been riding for two hours and you've only just noticed Lupus isn't with us.'

'That's because I've been thinking,' said Flavia, 'about how to rescue Popo.'

'No you haven't,' said Jonathan. 'You've been thinking about Flaccus and Prudentilla.'

Flavia glared at him and was about to make a cutting remark, but he looked so miserable that instead she said, 'What's wrong, Jonathan?'

After a long pause he spoke: 'I haven't been sleeping very well. Ever since we got back to Alexandria, I've . . .'

'What? You've what?'

'I haven't been sleeping very well.'

'Is it the voice you were telling us about?'

'That. And the dreams.'

'Dreams?'

He nodded. 'Last night I dreamt about the fire in Rome. For the third or fourth time this month.'

'I know,' said Flavia. 'The fire was terrible. I still have nightmares about it.'

'It's worse for me,' he said. 'Considering I started it.'

'You still feel guilty about what happened?'

'You could say that.' He gave a bitter laugh.

'But it wasn't really your fault.'

'Wasn't it?' They rode in silence for a while. Then Jonathan asked: 'Do you ever wonder why all these bad things have happened to us?'

'Of course,' said Flavia. 'I said in Alexandria that I wished I'd never become a detectrix. If we hadn't gone on that mission for the Emperor then maybe Popo wouldn't have been kidnapped.'

'It's not *your* fault,' said Jonathan. 'It's mine. Ever since the fire in Rome, we've had such bad luck.'

Flavia thought about this, then shook her head. 'No. The bad luck started before the fire. What about the dog-killer and the fever and the pirates? And don't forget Vesuvius!'

'Yes,' said Jonathan. 'I suppose you're right.'

But he did not sound convinced.

Lupus sat astride the bay mare in the shade of the cypress tree and watched the prophet baptise. The people stood in a group at the riverside, and when it was their turn one of the prophet's helpers would take them by the hand and lead them down through the reeds into the glittering water and take them to where Tychicus waited. The prophet stood waist deep in the water, holding his staff in his left hand.

The helper would take up position behind the person to be baptised. Tychicus would speak with the person, sometimes for quite a while. At last he would rest his right hand on the person's head, then push them under the water. His assistant would lift them up a moment later, then escort the dripping and spluttering convert back through the reeds to the river bank. He even baptised some lepers, and was not afraid to touch them.

Many of the freshly-baptised passed close to Lupus on their way back to town. He watched them closely. Some seemed dazed, others unaffected. But a few of them had looks of pure joy on their faces.

SCROLL XVII

It was almost dark as Nubia passed through the bedrooms, making sure all the children were tucked in.

She said goodnight to the four youngest girls last of all. Zoe was six, with straight dark hair and dark eyes. Larissa was also six. She had soft golden curls and brown eyes. Five-year-old Euodia had brown hair and hazel eyes, as did the youngest, Xanthia, only four years old.

'My bedroom is the one next door,' said Nubia, sitting on Xanthia's bed, 'so don't be afraid. I'll hear you if you call.' The little girl gazed up at her with long-lashed dark eyes full of trust and love.

Nubia leaned forward and kissed Xanthia on the forehead, the way her mother had kissed her when she was little. Then she stood and turned.

Aristo was leaning against the doorway, watching her. He must have been there for some time, for she had not been aware of his arrival. In the golden light from a small oil-lamp he looked tired but very handsome. His shoulder came away from the door-frame and he smiled at her, but his smile made the knife twist in her heart, so she looked away.

'You're so good with them,' he said softly, as she moved past him out into the colonnaded upper balcony. 'Already they love you.'

Nubia nodded and started towards the bedroom next door; it was small with two beds, one for her and one for Flavia. Nubia had chosen it for its frescoed blue panels with pigeons and doves.

'Play some music with me?' he said. 'I know you're tired. But I've missed it.'

Nubia turned and looked at him. In the twilight it was hard to make out the expression on his face.

'Perhaps we could play a lullaby to help them sleep?' he said.

'Yes,' said Nubia. 'I would like that.'

'Down in the palm tree courtyard?' he said. 'The jasmine is in bloom.'

'Yes,' she said, pulling the flute out from under the neck of her tunic.

Instead of starting downstairs, he stepped closer and gently took the flute from her fingers. 'This isn't yours,' he said, turning it in the half-light. 'It's a cheap reed flute. Where's your cherrywood flute? The one you got in Surrentum?'

He was standing so close that she could feel the heat from his body and smell his musky lavender scent. She kept her gaze on the floor, afraid that if she looked up her eyes would betray her feelings. 'I dedicated it to the god Neptune,' she said. 'As thanks for sending his dolphin to save me from the shipwreck.'

'A dolphin saved you?'

'Yes. When our ship ran aground in the storm.'

'You must tell me about it,' he said and put his hand on her shoulder. 'You poor thing. Even the memory of it is making you tremble.'

'Yes,' she said, 'I will tell you about the shipwreck and the dolphin after we have played lullaby music.'

She moved away. It was not the memories making her tremble. It was his touch.

Lupus had found a patch of lush grass beside the Little Maeander. He tethered the bay mare to a poplar tree, leaving enough rope to let her graze on the lush grass and drink from the river.

Then he went to spy on Tychicus, who was sitting near a fire with three of his helpers. They were eating flat bread and fish grilled on sticks. The smell made Lupus's stomach growl fiercely, but he ignored the hunger pangs.

It was dark now, and the night air carried the cool scent of the river. Lupus crept closer and listened to the prophet speaking with his friends. Tychicus had a deep, comforting voice, but the topic of discussion was not comforting. They were discussing the end of the world, and how quickly it would come.

Presently Tychicus rose and left the firelight for the darkness of the riverbank.

At first Lupus thought he had gone to relieve himself, but when the followers spread out their cloaks and lay down beside the dying embers of the fire, he realised this was the prophet's usual behaviour.

Using the starlight to light his way, he crept through the long grasses in the direction Tychicus had gone. There were tall poplar trees here by the river bank. Their leaves trembled in the warm night breeze. In the east, a silver glow on the horizon heralded the imminent appearance of the moon.

Then Lupus saw the prophet.

He was standing between two rows of poplars, leaning on his staff and gazing at the sky toward the east.

Lupus crept closer. Close enough to hear him praying in a strange bubbling language.

At last the moon appeared, a misshapen bowl of light rising behind distant mountains. The prophet's prayers became more urgent, more plaintive.

And now the moon was free of the horizon and as it floated up, the prophet slumped to the ground with a sigh, as if he had just won a great battle.

Lupus was about to go closer when he heard a twig crunch behind him.

He turned and his heart gave a lurching thud as he saw a huge dark shape emerge from behind a poplar tree.

The moon was up now and it clearly showed Lupus his mortal enemy. The light was so bright that he could even see the mark in the middle of the giant's forehead. It was the scar from a stone that Lupus had slung at the giant over a year ago. Now his enemy was advancing on him with a horrible grin.

Lupus groped for his sling belt. But he had lost it months earlier in the shipwreck, and anyway there were no stones here on the lush riverbank.

Lupus feinted one way, then darted the other, but it was no good. Ursus had anticipated his move and he grasped Lupus's wrist in an iron grip.

He was caught.

In a villa in Ephesus, forty-six children were lying clean and bathed in comfortable beds. Although their life had been terrible, it had held a sort of routine. Now everything had changed. The change had given them hope. And with hope came fear that their hope might be in vain.

Then the music began, lyre and flute blending together, rising up from the courtyard below and filling the rooms with a wordless song of comfort. The children had never heard such music before. It took them from their dark places and transported them to sun-dappled glades, with warm sunshine, cool breezes and birdsong. The notes were like a mother's fingers, gently brushing the hair from the forehead, soft and infinitely loving. And soon all the children were asleep.

SCROLL XVIII

On the right bank of the Little Maeander, Ursus was smothering Lupus in a bear hug.

'Nu gung hurd you,' the giant was saying. 'No gung hurd.'

It took a moment for Lupus to understand that the giant was trying to reassure him.

Lupus stopped struggling and Ursus released his grip. Lupus took a step back, but did not run away. Instead, he stared at the giant in disbelief. He had always assumed that Ursus was mute, but now he was talking.

The giant was on his knees, so that his big head was level with Lupus's. 'Nod gung hurd you,' he repeated. 'Didn mean do scare you. Sorry.' His eyes were wet.

Without taking his eyes from Ursus, Lupus shrugged with his palms up, to say: Why?

Ursus frowned. 'I dond unnersdan,' he said thickly.

Lupus pulled out his wax tablet, flipped it open and with a trembling hand wrote: WHY ARE YOU BEING NICE? WHERE IS MINDIUS AND BABY? Then he held it up so that the light from the moon shone on it.

Ursus shook his head. 'Cand read,' he said. 'Sorry. Didn mean do scare or hurd you. Sorry. Will you furgive me?'

Frowning, Lupus put his wax tablet away. Again he made the gesture asking: Why?

'Why am I sorry?' said Ursus. 'Why am I gud now?'

Lupus nodded.

Ursus gave a radiant smile. 'Becuz Ive been forgiven and Ive been healed.' He stuck out his tongue and pointed at it. 'Ive been healed and wand you do know. You can be healed, doo!'

In the palm tree courtyard of the Villa Vinea, Nubia finished telling Aristo about her adventures in North Africa and Egypt.

'Amazing,' he kept saying. 'That's amazing.'

The jasmine-scented courtyard was dimly lit by bronze hanging lamps, some of them were reflected in the mirror smooth pool beside them. The silver light of the rising moon illuminated the tops of the four palm trees.

'Tomorrow,' said Aristo softly, 'I am going to gather all the children together and begin to teach them. It's what I know how to do, and it will keep them busy and occupied. Do you think that's a good idea?'

'Yes,' said Nubia. 'That is a very good idea. You are a wonderful teacher, Aristo.'

The air was filled with the scent of jasmine, but as he moved a little closer she caught a subtle whiff of his musky lavender scent. It made her dizzy.

'Nubia,' he said softly. 'I want to tell you something.'

The tone of his voice made her heart begin to pound.

'Something you said a few days ago . . . about being old enough for love . . . For a long time I thought . . . But then Flavia said . . . and I couldn't bear to think . . . I've been such a fool . . .'

Nubia couldn't understand what he was saying. So she willed the pulsing roar in her ears to be quiet and when it was, she heard him say: 'I loved Miriam so much!'

Nubia felt sick. How could she compete with the most beautiful girl in the Roman Empire? A girl whose beauty would never fade or grow wrinkled?

She had been right not to tell Aristo her feelings. He would laugh at her. Or despise her. Or worst of all: pity her.

In the darkness she felt him take her hand in his. The shock of his touch was so powerful that she almost cried out.

'You're trembling again,' he said. 'Are you cold?'

'No,' she whispered. She wanted to cry out: *Why do you still love Miriam? She never loved you. But I do. I will always love you.*

But she knew it would be the worst thing she could do.

So instead she snatched her hand from his and ran upstairs and groped her way along the dim corridor to the bedroom and threw herself onto the bed.

And in the lonely darkness, she wept.

'Ursus?' said the prophet, rising up from the damp grass. 'What are you doing here? And who is the boy?'

'Fwend,' said Ursus in his thick voice. 'My fwend. Will oo pray for him?'

Tychicus sighed. He looked dazed and tired.

'Yes, of course I'll pray for your friend,' he said. 'Leave us, Ursus. Go. Sleep. I will pray for your friend.'

Ursus nodded and said to Lupus, 'I will waid by yur

horse. I will look afder her. Dond wand bad people to sdeal her.'

Lupus nodded. His mind was spinning like a lump of clay on a potter's wheel. Ursus was healed! He could speak. Could Tychicus heal him, too?

As Ursus disappeared into the shadows, Tychicus turned to Lupus.

'Don't be afraid,' he said. 'I sense the Spirit of God in you. But it is struggling with another spirit. The spirit of fear and pain. Let me pray for you. Here, let us sit on the grass.'

Lupus grunted and sat on the lush grass beside the prophet.

The man sat cross-legged and laid his hand on Lupus's head. Then he closed his eyes and began muttering in his strange language. 'I see a wolf cub,' he said presently. 'It is trying to howl in pain but it has no voice.'

Lupus swallowed hard and his eyes swam with tears. How could the prophet know this? Had Ursus told him?

The prophet opened his eyes. 'What is your name boy?'

Lupus pulled out his wax tablet and wrote: LUPUS. I AM MUTE.

The moonlight showed his words clearly.

'Ah,' said Tychicus. 'Ah.' He closed his eyes again and after a time he said: 'I see you in a great arena. You are praying to God.'

Lupus uttered an involuntary gasp. A year and a half ago, when Jonathan had been tied to a stake in the Flavian amphitheatre at Rome, Lupus had promised God to serve him all his life if Jonathan lived. And Jonathan had been spared.

'And now I see you in a boat, surrounded by a great

expanse of water.' The prophet opened his eyes and looked at Lupus in surprise. 'The Lord has spoken to you. You know his voice.'

Lupus nodded. The tears were running down his face, hot and wet.

The prophet closed his eyes again. 'And I see monsters sculpted from sand. They stand on the shore. But the power of God's love, like wind and sea, is melting them to nothing.'

Lupus nodded again, numbly. This man was telling him his whole life. Things he had never told anyone else, not even his friends.

The prophet opened his eyes. They were no longer far-seeing. They were focused on Lupus, full of warmth and love. 'You know all these things. You know the power of forgiveness and you know the power of God's love. There remains only one thing.'

Lupus looked at him, wide-eyed, ready to do anything.

'You must die to yourself,' said Tychicus, 'so that you can be born from above. Are you ready to be baptised?'

Lupus nodded. He was ready to be baptised. And to be healed.

Tychicus used his walking stick to push himself up. Then he transferred the stick to his left hand and helped Lupus up with his right. 'Come,' he said, still holding Lupus's hand. 'Here is the river; here am I, and here are you. And God is always with us. Does anything prevent us?'

Jonathan watched the lopsided moon swim up into a sky full of stars.

A few hours earlier, at dusk, he and Flavia had finally

caught up with Bato and his two soldiers at a clearing near the river. The soldiers had cheerfully shared their campfire and their rations. Jonathan and Flavia contributed grapes pulled from the vineyards and a bag of sunflower seeds.

The night was warm and the grass thick, and now all the others were asleep. Even Flavia was snoring gently. From time to time, one of the horses would snort softly in the darkness. Jonathan remembered another time when they had slept beside a river, on the way to Athens.

On that occasion he had thought himself pursued by Furies. He smiled bitterly. He would almost prefer the mythical snake-haired demons to this taunting relentless voice. Every day it seemed to grow stronger, more powerful. It was talking to him now. When had it started?

He knew immediately. It had started in Alexandria the day Aristo had arrived with news of Popo's abduction. That's when the voice had started.

He wished he could be back in Alexandria, in that clean marble city of wide streets and pure air. Perhaps the City of God – the new Jerusalem – would be like that. He remembered vaguely seeing such a city once in his dreams.

But now the voice was reminding him that if God really did exist, and if he had prepared a city in Paradise, then Jonathan deserved no part of it.

'**You started the fire**,' said the voice. '**You are a mass murderer and you deserve to suffer. The place reserved for you is the garbage tip, Gehenna, where rubbish is burned for eternity.**'

★

The prophet led Lupus down to the Little Maeander. It was transformed by the moon's light into a dazzling milky path, snaking away to the northeast.

Tychicus stepped in first and Lupus followed, pushing the reeds aside. The cool river mud squelched into his sandals and between his toes, but it was not unpleasant. The water was also cool, but warmer than the mud. As he followed the prophet, it swirled around his calves, then his knees, then his thighs, then his waist. When the water was up to Lupus's chest, Tychicus stopped.

He turned and faced Lupus.

'Do you know why we do this?'

Lupus shook his head.

'It symbolises cleansing from our sins. A sin is anything we do that disappoints God or hurts our fellow man. Do you repent of all the sins you have ever committed?'

Lupus thought for a moment, then shrugged and grunted yes.

'Good. Then sin will no longer be your master. Do you accept Jesus as your lord, just as a slave would obey a new master?'

Lupus grunted yes.

The prophet gestured at the water. 'Baptism also symbolises our death and rebirth. It is as if we go down to our grave and rise up again. We die to our old sinful life and are born anew to serve our new master. Are you ready?'

For a third time, Lupus grunted yes.

Tychicus laid his right hand on the top of Lupus's head.

'Then in the name of God the Father, God the Son and God the Holy Spirit, I baptise you, Lupus.'

As Tychicus gently pushed on Lupus's head, he let himself sink down beneath the shimmering skin of the river into the blackness beneath. The water swallowed him, and for a moment he imagined he was dead. Then Tychicus grasped the back of his tunic and pulled him up and Lupus rose gasping in to the cool thyme-scented night with its milky river and sky full of stars. The world felt clean and fresh and new. He felt different, too.

His heart pounding with hope, Lupus put his finger inside his mouth to see if he had been healed.

A moment later he opened his tongueless mouth and howled.

SCROLL XIX

'Wait, Lupus!' cried Tychicus. 'Come back!'

But Lupus did not stop. He splashed through the black water to the left bank and ran up through dark reeds and squelching mud until he reached firmer ground.

Even then he did not stop running. He left the lush grass behind, and ran into the scrubby plain full of rocks and dirt and prickly shrubs. Lit by moonlight, the world was black and white. Several times he fell, but he continued to run blindly.

God knew everything about him. God had told the prophet his life. Lupus had been willing to die and be reborn. He was willing to serve God's son as a slave served a master. But despite all this, God had not deemed Lupus worthy to be healed.

Lupus howled again with rage and anguish.

And finally he collapsed among the thorns and thistles, scratched and bruised and in a deeper agony of his soul than he had ever felt before.

In his vision he sees arrowhead-shaped stars creep into the constellation of Aquarius, the water bearer. Some of the arrowheads collide with others and silent puffs of light are followed by darkness. The battling stars move slowly but he knows this is only an illusion because they are so far away. He knows they are immensely huge and unimaginably fast. And suddenly he understands. They are angels and demons, battling over the souls of men in the heavenly realms.

Lupus woke at dawn to find himself being carried like a baby in the arms of a gentle giant. Birds were singing and the pure air was cool. The sun warmed his face and he looked up to see Ursus. The giant was weeping. His hot fat tears splashed onto Lupus's tunic.

'Sorry,' he said. 'I'm sorry, Lupus. I wanded him do heal you, doo.'

Lupus nodded. He felt empty and sad, but touched to see his former enemy weeping.

He patted Ursus on his massive chest, but this only made the giant weep more. They had reached the riverbank now, and the sun was making the poplar trees throw long cool shadows across the dew-drenched grass.

Ursus put Lupus down beside his mare. Nearby was the black gelding from Halicarnassus.

One of Tychicus's assistants from the day before was taking a feedbag from its head.

'They've been fed and brushed,' said the youth to Ursus. 'Tychicus says the man you are looking for lives in a rustic villa about five miles from here. Take the road south towards Halicarnassus. About two miles out of the city, you'll reach a fork, take the road on the right. It's another two or three miles. Up in the hills. Ask for the Fisherman.'

Ursus nodded at him and looked down at Lupus. 'We are going do see a man even greader than Dychicus. He will heal your dung. Will you come?'

After a moment's thought, Lupus nodded. Then he raised his eyebrows, as if to say: *Who?*

'He knew Jesus when he lived in dis world,' said Ursus. 'And saw him afder he came back from da dead. If anyone can heal you, he can.'

They rode for an hour – Lupus on his bay mare, Ursus on his black gelding – up into the mountains, and in the green hills three miles south of Ephesus they came to a rustic villa surrounded by trees.

They dismounted at the front gate, and Ursus said to the doorkeeper, 'Dychicus send us do see da Fisherman.'

The gate swung open and they led their horses in. A one-storey complex of buildings formed three sides of a square around a farm courtyard and vegetable garden. Chickens pecked in the dust and a white-bearded old slave in a knitted skullcap stood in a bean patch, digging with his hoe. Lupus also saw onions, cucumbers and melons.

There was a trough of water with posts nearby, so they tethered the two horses there, and let them drink.

'Greetings,' said a youth, running up to them. 'May the Lord be with you.'

'And also wid you,' replied Ursus. 'We seek da Fisherman.'

From the bean patch the old bearded slave stopped digging. 'I am he,' he said in accented Greek. 'I am the Fisherman.'

With a cry, Ursus ran to the old man, knelt and began to kiss his feet.

'No, no!' chuckled the man. 'Do not worship me. I am a child of God, as you are. Besides, it tickles. Also, you are trampling my beans. Come, get up. What is your name?'

'I am Ursus and dis is Lupus. Dychicus send us.'

'Ah. Tychicus. I hear he is baptising not far from here. Ask him why he has not come to see his old friend.'

'He begs you do pray for dis boy. He has no dung.'

The old man left his hoe leaning against the bean trellis and came over to Lupus. He had an eagle's-beak nose, bushy white eyebrows and keen black eyes. He put his calloused hand lightly on Lupus's shoulder. 'So, you have no tongue?'

Lupus shook his head.

'What is his name?'

'His name is Lupus,' said Ursus.

'Ah, Lupus. The wolf.' The old man chuckled again. 'My name is Yohanan ben Zabdai. Some call me the Fisherman and some called me Ioannes, but you can call me John. I was one of Jesus' twelve disciples.'

Flavia groaned as she swung her leg over her horse's back.

They had woken at cockcrow, breakfasted on cold bits of grilled sheep entrails and now they were setting off on what promised to be the hottest day of the year. Her limbs ached and her bottom was impossibly sore.

'Remind me why we're doing this?' she muttered. She was really speaking to herself but Jonathan answered.

'I'm not sure why *I'm* doing it,' he said, 'but you obviously have something to prove.' He kicked Tiberina hard in the flanks. 'Come on, you old piece of horse-meat,' he said angrily.

'Jonathan, we've been in bad situations before but you've never been so bad-tempered. What's wrong? Is it the voice? The dreams?'

'I don't mind the dreams,' he said.

'But the voice. You do mind that.'

He stared resolutely ahead, his jaw clenched.

'Why has it started now?' she asked. 'The fire was a year and a half ago.'

'I don't know!' he snapped, and then added, 'I wish I did.'

'Is there anything I can do to help? To make it better?'

Jonathan gave a bitter smile and shook his head. Flavia sighed deeply and they rode together in silence for a while, following Bato and the two soldiers, and squinting into the rising sun.

Presently Jonathan said, 'Before we moved to Ostia, we used to live in Rome, in one of those big apartment blocks. The latrines were downstairs, right at the bottom. One evening before bed, I was sitting there and I saw a bug on the floor. Just a little one. But one of its legs had been crushed and it was crawling in a circle around its leg. It was obviously in agony, going around and around in pain.'

'Did you put it out of its misery?' asked Flavia, glancing over at him. Beneath his straw sunhat, his profile was grim.

'No. I couldn't bear the thought of it smeared on the bottom of my sandal. I thought it would be dead soon anyway.'

'Poor thing.'

'The next morning I went back to the latrines. And it was still there, still alive, still going around in circles. It had been struggling in agony all night.'

'Oh, how terrible!'

'For such a little insect that night must have seemed like a lifetime.'

'I know.'

'People are like that.'

'What do you mean?'

'People. Humans. We're wounded and in pain and we go in circles on the floor of life's latrine, never achieving anything. Waiting for God to bring down his foot and put us out of our misery by squashing us.'

'Oh Jonathan, what an awful thing to say.'

'It's true,' he said. 'What's the point of life anyway? We're born, we struggle, and then we die. What's the point?'

Lupus, Ursus and the old man called John were eating breakfast at a wooden table in the shade of a mulberry tree.

John had taken off his skullcap to reveal a bald head fringed by white hair. Then he had pronounced a blessing over a frugal breakfast of white cheese, olives and cucumber. He had given Lupus a ceramic beaker with a salty yoghurt drink.

As Lupus carefully tipped the drink down his throat, he secretly examined John. With his hooked nose, keen eyes and beetling brows, the old fisherman looked like an eagle. But he radiated gentleness and love. The farm cat was rubbing itself against John's legs and on the table, sparrows pecked crumbs only inches from his hands. One of the sparrows fluttered up to John's shoulder and the sight was so extraordinary that Lupus choked on his last swallow of liquid yogurt. Ursus pounded Lupus on the back while John refilled Lupus's beaker from the jug and handed it to him.

Lupus drank down half the beaker, then nodded his thanks. His eyes were still watering and his convulsions had frightened away the cat and the sparrows.

'Beloveds,' said the fisherman when they had finished eating, 'what can I do for you?'

Lupus wrote on his wax tablet: CAN YOU HEAL ME?

'I can do nothing apart from God,' said John.

Lupus rubbed out one word and replaced it with another: CAN GOD HEAL ME?

'God can do anything. But are you sure you want your tongue back?'

Lupus nodded.

'Of course he duz,' said Ursus defensively. 'Why wouldn he?'

Lupus frowned down at the table. He remembered the strange half-dream he had experienced: of something huge and hot and wet in his mouth, choking him, suffocating him. Would it feel like that if his tongue grew back? Would he even be able to talk? Or would he have to learn to speak again, like a baby?

'In the resurrection,' said John, 'we will be whole and healthy, forever. This life and its suffering lasts but the blink of an eye.'

Lupus frowned. He wasn't sure he understood.

'God knows the plans he has for you,' said John. 'Plans to prosper you and not to harm you. Plans to give you a hope and future. Above all, know that he loves you, Lupus, with infinite love.'

Ursus beamed at Lupus. 'God loves you,' he said. 'And he loves me, doo.'

John nodded happily. 'Tell me, beloveds,' he said. 'You

have both been baptised in water. But have you received the baptism of the Holy Spirit?'

Lupus shook his head and looked at John wide-eyed.

'And you, Ursus?'

'No.' The big man looked puzzled.

'Then let me pray for you now.'

SCROLL XX

Lupus stood in the shade of the mulberry tree before John the fisherman. Ursus stood on Lupus's other side. The old man had one hand raised high, resting on the giant's head, and one hand low, on Lupus's head.

Lupus closed his eyes as the old fisherman prayed. 'Father God, come and fill your beloved children with your Holy Spirit.' Then John began to pray in a language like none Lupus had ever heard.

There was a thud beside Lupus and he opened one eye to see Ursus lying on the ground at his feet. A beatific smile spread across the giant's face.

Lupus was wondering how he could ask John what had happened when he felt a kind of pressure, as if he stood at the bottom of a great warm ocean: an infinite ocean of God's love. The pressure was too great for him to stand and a moment later he found himself on his back beside Ursus, looking up into the leaves of the mulberry tree, feeling great waves of love washing through him.

It was the most glorious thing he had ever felt. As if he were lying in the palm of God's strong, warm hand. He never wanted this feeling to end. He would lie here forever.

He began to laugh, and beside him Ursus laughed. And above them the Fisherman laughed, too.

Nubia stood in the shaded colonnade of the Orpheus courtyard and watched Aristo teach. He had spread reed mats for the younger children and put chairs at the back for the older ones. He was sitting on one of the cedarwood benches beneath the fig tree, using the dolls Nubia and Flavia had made to act out a Greek myth. Three more children had been reunited with their families early that morning, but there were still forty-three children here at the Villa Vinea, aged between four and thirteen. They all sat watching him.

Nubia watched him, too, her heart full of pride: Aristo the storyteller. He was so good at this. These damaged children, who had been beaten and abused, were enthralled as he related the Greek myth about the abduction of Persephone.

When he reached the part of the story where Pluto came up from the underworld and snatched young Persephone as she was gathering violets, two of the younger girls began to cry. Nubia moved silently forward and sat between them. Euodia from Laodicea hugged her arm and grew silent. But golden-haired Larissa kept sobbing. Nubia let her cry, but she kept her hand on the girl's back. She knew what a release tears could bring. Next to her, Sapphira was holding little Xanthia in her lap. Her face showed no emotion.

Aristo stopped speaking for a moment and looked at Nubia, his eyebrows slightly raised in query. She smiled and gave him a little nod in return, and he continued.

When it came time in Aristo's story for Demeter to

descend to Hades to plead for her daughter, he used the Nubia doll.

'*Let my daughter go!*' Aristo made Demeter say. '*She is not made for this world of darkness, but for the world of flowers and sunshine and joy.*'

'*Very well,*' said the dark-haired Pluto doll, one of Flavia's efforts which had gone wrong. '*But she must spend part of every year down here with me, for she ate six pomegranate seeds in my court.*'

Larissa looked up at Nubia through her tears. 'Did Sefunny have to go back down?'

'Yes,' said Nubia and handed her a handkerchief. 'Persephone had to go back down to darkness.'

'Will I?' asked Larissa.

'I hope not,' said Nubia, and kissed the top of her head. 'But if you do, remember: you are made for a world of sunshine and flowers. And it's always here waiting for you.'

'Will you stay here with me?' asked Larissa.

Nubia lifted her head to look at Aristo. 'Yes,' she said. 'I will stay with you as long as I can.'

It was late afternoon and Jonathan's whole body ached from all the riding he had done over the past few days, but he endured each jolt and bounce as penance for his crime. Bato and his two soldiers had made them ride hard all day, only stopping briefly at noon to eat a handful of grapes and let the horses drink from the river.

Their determination had paid off: around the fourth hour after noon, two men on donkeys told Bato they had seen a man and a woman on horseback only half an hour before. The man had fit Mindius's description and the woman had been carrying a baby.

If only I could rescue Popo, thought Jonathan, maybe the guilt would go away.

Do you think saving one baby will help? said the voice. **You killed thousands. You deserve to die like that insect on the floor.**

'But the fire was an accident,' muttered Jonathan under his breath. 'Like Flavia said.'

Only at the very last moment, said the voice. **Until then you wanted to help the zealot destroy Rome. You know you did.**

'I didn't know the wind would change. I only wanted to kill Titus, not all those innocent people.'

But you did kill innocent people, said the voice. **Twenty thousand of them**.

As Jonathan rode through vineyards lit emerald green by the late afternoon sunlight, he knew the voice was right.

'Maybe I should die,' he whispered. 'And take Mindius with me.'

For a moment the voice fell silent and even the jarring of his mount no longer hurt. He inhaled the strong smell of horse, underlain with the fragrant scent of thyme, and listened to the throb of the cicadas in the vines. The sun was warm on his back and there was a taste of dust in his mouth. He spat onto the road, then took a swig of sweet warm water from his gourd.

For a few glorious moments he felt empty and clean and free.

Then the voice returned.

Burn. You deserve to burn, too.

He wanted to scream in frustration, but then they rounded a bend in the road and Jonathan saw one of the most amazing sights of his life: on the mountain straight ahead was a cliff gleaming whiter than any marble he had ever seen. And a city stood above it.

'Hierapolis,' said one of Bato's soldiers from his horse. 'The holy city.'

'Great Juno's peacock!' breathed Flavia an hour later. She reined in Herodotus beside Bato's mount. 'It's covered with snow in the middle of August.'

The dazzling slope was on the left hand side of the road. Up close she could see what seemed to be frozen waterfalls pouring out of scallop-shaped pools, dozens of them, mounting the side of the mountain like semi-circular stairs. Behind them the sun was setting, and the frozen water gleamed golden in its light. There was the soft constant murmur of rushing waters.

'It can't be snow or ice,' said Jonathan, as his horse came up beside hers. 'It's as hot as Hades today. And if it was covered with snow, we'd be able to feel the coolness from here.'

Bato looked at one of his soldiers. 'You've been here before, Demetrius. What makes it look that way? Is it an illusion?'

'Hot springs near the top of the cliff,' said Demetrius, the soldier with the fierce blue eyes. 'Something in the water makes them grow hard, like frozen waterfalls. Only they're warm, not cold. People say the water is sacred, with healing properties.'

'It's beautiful!' breathed Flavia.

'I've never seen anything like it,' said Jonathan.

Demetrius pointed up towards the top of the dazzling rank of cascades. 'The town itself is up there. It was badly damaged in an earthquake ten years ago. But they've rebuilt most of it. My girlfriend's mother used to have a bad rash,' he added. 'She bathed in these waters and now her skin is as smooth as a baby's.'

Bato nodded absently. He was scanning the scalloped steps of the cliffs. There was a woman washing her clothes in one pool, and three men ritually rising and bending over another further up. A mule-cart was clopping up the road, and a litter carried by four slaves was coming down towards them. Apart from that, there was nobody around.

Then Bato cocked his head. 'Listen! Did you hear that? A horse's whinny.' He pointed to the pines on the right side of the road. 'Coming from those woods.'

'Yes!' cried Flavia. And without waiting for permission she heeled Herodotus into motion and rode into the woods.

Bato and his men galloped after Flavia but, as usual, Tiberina refused to be hurried.

'Come on, you old nag!' Jonathan kicked her hard in the flanks.

The mare sighed and started up the path after the others.

At that moment something on the sparkling mountain to his left caught Jonathan's eye. Two figures had appeared from behind one of the frozen waterfalls: a man and a woman, bathed in orange by the setting sun, picking their way carefully across the pools. The woman wore a headscarf and carried a baby. He could hear its thin wail.

It had to be Mindius, Lydia and Popo. And they were only two or three hundred feet away.

Jonathan reined in Tiberina.

'Lydia!' he shouted, waving his arm. 'Lydia! Over here!'

The washerwoman and the three bathers turned to look at him, but the man and woman with the baby did not seem to hear.

'Mindius!' he shouted.

This time the man and the woman both turned to look at him. The man was Mindius all right; Jonathan recognised him from the portrait in his Halicarnassus villa. But he would not have known Lydia. Her face was thinner and she seemed to have aged ten years. Her blue eyes were dark with grief.

'The brute,' muttered Jonathan.

The baby was still crying.

'Mindius!' called Jonathan. 'Let them go! There are soldiers after you. They'll be here any moment!' He turned towards the woods. 'Flavia! Bato! I've found him! He's over here!'

But there was no reply from the woods and now Mindius had grasped the woman's hand and was pulling her after him across one of the pools.

'Mindius!' shouted Jonathan, riding up to the edge of the pools. 'Don't do it! You can't escape!'

But Mindius *was* escaping. Jonathan looked back towards the woods, but there was still no sign of Bato or Flavia or the two soldiers.

With a curse, Jonathan dismounted.

SCROLL XXI

'Lupus!' cried Nubia, putting her piece of bread down on the mat and rising to her feet. 'Behold! You are back. Did you find baby Popo?'

It was evening and all the children were sitting beneath the grape arbour in the canal garden having a picnic dinner of bread and thyme-scented honey. Lupus had come into the green garden, followed by a bald old man with a white beard.

Nubia ran to him. 'Did you find Popo?'

Lupus shook his head, but his eyes were shining. He held up his wax tablet, then pointed to the old man, who was gazing at the children in delight.

'John?' read Nubia. 'Prophet and friend of Jesus?'

Lupus nodded and began to laugh. The old man named John chuckled, too.

Nubia stared at Lupus. Something was different about him. She had never seen him like this. Then she gasped as a third figure stepped out of the shaded corridor into the garden. She took an involuntary step backwards and bumped into Aristo, who had come to stand behind her.

The man who had emerged from the corridor was an ugly giant, with a broken nose, close-set eyes and a scar in the middle of his forehead. The last time she had seen him, he had been running like a madman from the theatre at Halicarnassus, yelling incoherently.

With a cry of horror, Nubia turned to hide her face in Aristo's tunic, and she felt his strong arms encircle her protectively. The giant was Mindius's evil bodyguard, Ursus.

The cherry-red sun was sinking in the west, bathing the calcite steps beneath Hierapolis in a pink light and making their scallop pools glow orange. Mindius was picking his way across this alien landscape, one hand out for balance, the other gripping the girl's hand. Jonathan could hear the baby crying above the murmur of rushing water: his little nephew Popo.

Somehow Jonathan had taken a different route across the slope and now he faced a six-foot gap between two pools, with a twenty-foot plunge between. A gust of wind snatched Jonathan's straw sunhat and spun it away. His stomach writhed as the hat rolled down from one cascade to another, and finally to the gleaming floor hundreds of feet below.

Jonathan forced himself to focus on his prey. He saw Mindius looking back at him: 'Who are you? What do you want?' came the man's angry voice above the rushing waters.

'I want my . . . nephew back!' Jonathan tried to shout but he was wheezing. 'And I want you . . . to pay for . . . what you've done!'

Mindius frowned in puzzlement, then shook his head in disgust and continued on up the slope, pulling the girl and the baby after him.

Jonathan almost cried with frustration. His sister Miriam had died so that her twins might live, and now this monster was about to sacrifice one of them. The baby's cry made him angry and the anger gave him strength. Without thinking, Jonathan leapt the gap between the two pools.

He managed the leap, but his foot slipped and he fell forward into the steaming water. It was only a few inches deep and the water was not boiling, just the temperature of a warm bath. But now his sandals were too slippery to wear. As he unlaced them, an idea occurred to him. He pulled one off and threw it at Mindius. It splashed harmlessly. Jonathan took aim and threw the second sandal, giving it a spin. It missed Mindius but struck the girl's leg. She cried out and Jonathan saw Mindius turn and look back, his eyes wild. He said something to the girl and they began to run.

Jonathan ran, too.

Abruptly, the girl slipped and fell backwards into one of the pools. The baby was crying lustily now. Mindius cursed and went back for them.

The surreal pink and orange world of frozen waterfalls blurred as tears of frustration filled Jonathan's eyes. He blinked them away and the world cleared.

But Mindius had disappeared.

And now Lydia was screaming.

'Stay there!' cried Jonathan. 'I'm coming!'

As he came closer he saw what had happened. Mindius had slipped and was hanging from the slippery lip of one of the calcified waterfalls. Jonathan came wheezing up and looked over the side. The drop was only fifteen or twenty feet, but the ledge below was not wide and from there the slippery slope tumbled down for hundreds of feet.

'Help me!' cried Mindius in Latin. 'Help me, boy!' His accent was just like Jonathan's father's and this disconcerted Jonathan for a moment. Then he remembered. Mindius was also Jewish.

Lydia was sobbing now and little Popo was still crying, his wails echoing eerily off the strange formations around them, now blood red in the light of the dying sun.

'No,' said Jonathan. 'I won't help you. You're a murderer and you deserve to die. As Seneca says: "The way to freedom is over a cliff." So be free.'

He turned his back on Mindius and went to help Lydia and his baby nephew.

'Ursus!' cried Nubia, withdrawing from Aristo's arms. 'You were Magnus's henchman.'

'Yes,' said the big man, hanging his ugly head. 'And Mindius's, doo.'

'You did bad things.' Nubia turned and gave Lupus a reproachful look. 'Lupus, how could you bring him here?'

'Do not be angry with the boy,' said the old man called John. 'Ursus here has repented. He has asked God's forgiveness. Can't you see he's sorry for what he did? Little children, let us love one another.'

Lupus nodded enthusiastically.

Aristo narrowed his eyes at Ursus. 'You repented?'

'What is repent?' asked Nubia.

'*Metanoia*,' chuckled the man with the white beard. 'Change of mind. It's when you turn your life around and go in a new direction.'

Ursus looked up eagerly. 'Yes! I am going a new way. I repended and God healed me. Gave me my dung.'

'Your what?' said Nubia.

Lupus grinned and pointed into his mouth.

'My dung.'

'I think he means tongue,' said Aristo, and then to Ursus. 'You were mute?'

Ursus nodded.

'Like Lupus?' said Nubia. She was aware of all the children behind her.

'Yes,' said Ursus.

'Your tongue was cut out and then it grew back?' said Aristo.

Ursus frowned and shook his head. 'My dung was burned when I was liddle. Never could speag.'

'When were you healed?' Nubia asked Ursus.

'In Halicarnassus,' said Ursus. 'In da dee ah dur.'

Nubia and Aristo frowned at one another.

Lupus wrote on his wax tablet: THEATRE

'In the theatre!' cried Aristo. 'The day we saw you running and yelling?'

'Yez,' said Ursus. 'I wuz yelling for joy. Run do dell Minduz. He came do see proffid and he repended, doo.'

'Mindius repented?' breathed Nubia.

'Yes,' said Ursus happily. 'Mindius repended, doo. He vows do be good, now. Jusd like me. The proffid healed him, doo.'

SCROLL XXII

Lupus turned and stared in disbelief at Ursus: Mindius had repented?

'Wool fluff!' said Aristo. 'If Mindius had repented then he wouldn't have kidnapped Miriam's baby.'

They were still standing in the canal garden, in the cool of the evening. Behind them, thirty-nine children were watching.

Ursus frowned and shook his big head. 'Mindius duz nod kidnap babies. He only dakes children. Bud nod any more. Now he is gud.' Ursus looked over Aristo's shoulder at the children. 'He renounced his evil ways. He is sorry.'

'But he kidnapped Popo,' said Aristo. 'Do you deny that?'

'Who?'

'Popo. Philadelphus. The baby from Ostia. And his nursemaid, Lydia,' said Aristo. 'If Mindius had repented he wouldn't have kidnapped them.'

'Mindius didn kidnap baby.'

'Then why did he ride off with them?' asked Aristo.

Ursus's crinkled forehead relaxed. 'Oh! Dad baby.' He looked at Lupus. 'Dad baby you saw when we ride fasd?'

Lupus nodded.

'That was Popo, wasn't it?' said Nubia.

'No!' Ursus chuckled. 'Dad baby is Mindius's baby. Chloe one of his girls and baby is his baby.'

'But,' stammered Aristo, 'When Bato asked Magnus the dwarf if it was Miriam's baby, he said yes. Magnus said Mindius planned to sacrifice it.'

Ursus shook his head angrily. 'Magnus da dwarf is a big fad liar,' he said. 'He probably sez dad for revenge on you.'

Lupus stared wide-eyed at Nubia and then at Aristo.

All this time they had been pursuing the wrong baby.

The slave-trader Mindius was hanging from the calcite cliff and begging for help, but Jonathan ignored him and went to help Lydia.

'Stay away from me!' cried the woman. 'Stay away from my baby!' As she twisted away from him, her headscarf slipped to her shoulders.

Jonathan stared in disbelief: the girl was not blue-eyed, fair-haired Lydia. This woman had dark eyes and hair. He looked down at the crying baby. It was not Popo.

'Help me, for the love of God!' cried Mindius. 'Can't hold on much longer.'

Jonathan turned and looked back down at Mindius and for the first time he saw him up close. He saw that Mindius had unusually hairy ears and that his skin still had a sickly yellow tinge from an excess of bile.

The revelation came to Jonathan like a thunderbolt from a blue sky.

Mindius was like Midas.

Midas, with his satyrs' ears and golden touch, the king brought down by hubris. Mindius was Midas, and Midas was the Key.

'If you let me die,' grunted Mindius, 'then my blood will be on your hands.'

But Jonathan was already stepping forward and extending his right hand.

Mindius grasped it with his left and started to pull himself up. But his foot must have slipped for Jonathan felt himself suddenly jerked forward.

Time seemed to slow as he pitched forward over the curved lip of the pool, towards Mindius's horrified face. And now he was falling, they were falling, Jonathan and his enemy: falling together.

'If the baby wasn't kidnapped,' said Aristo to Ursus, 'why was Mindius fleeing with it?'

'Baby was son of girl Mindius dook from Smyrna. Baby has derrible rash over skin. Mindius is sick, doo. He has yellow skin, yellow eyes. When I dell him proffid healed me, Mindius dakes girl and baby and we ride fasd as we can do see proffid.'

Lupus looked up in surprise and began to write on his wax tablet.

Aristo leant forward and read it out loud: *'When I saw you riding away, you were going to see the prophet?'*

'Yez!' Ursus nodded at Lupus. 'For proffid do heal baby. Bud crowds are big and someone dells us wrong way becuz dey all hade Mindius. We ride and ride and den durn around and ride back again and finally we find him on hillside. We hear him preach and see him heal people. We sday wid him and finally he prays for Mindius and Chloe and for da baby. Den he says go dip baby in holy pools of Hierapolis and he will be healed.'

'So that's why Mindius and the girl are going to

Hierapolis,' said Aristo. 'They're not running away. They're running towards.'

'Mindius is trying to help the baby,' said Nubia.

'But why?' said Aristo.

'Because he repended,' said Ursus patiently, as if to a small child. 'Now he is gud.'

Beside him white-bearded John nodded. 'There is great rejoicing in heaven,' he said, 'when such a sinner repents.'

'Don't move,' came the man's voice in Jonathan's ear, above the sound of rushing waters. 'Don't move or we're both dead.'

Jonathan opened his eyes to a vast sky. He slowly turned his head and his stomach writhed at the precipitous drop below: a tumbling, slippery slope of crystalline rock, pink in the light of the setting sun. He was lying in two inches of warm water. And a man was embracing him from behind. Mindius.

Couldn't even do a proper job of killing yourself, said the voice in Jonathan's head.

'If you move,' said Mindius. 'We'll both go over the edge and fall down the mountain.' There was a strained note in his voice, he seemed to be in pain.

'The world would be a better place without either of us,' said Jonathan. But he lay still, his heart pounding and his body trembling.

'What on earth can you have done that was so terrible?' said Mindius. 'You can't be much more than thirteen.'

Around them the waters sighed and muttered.

Go on, said the voice. **Tell him.**

'I started a fire in Rome that killed twenty thousand people.'

Mindius was silent for a few moments.

Then he chuckled.

'Why are you laughing?' said Jonathan. His left ankle began to throb. He must have twisted it in the fall.

'And I thought *I* was a sinner,' he said.

Jonathan stiffened and Mindius tightened his grip. 'Before you kill us both,' he said softly, 'hear me out.'

Don't listen to him, said the voice. But Jonathan had no choice.

'Do you think you deserve to die?' said Mindius.

'We probably *are* going to die,' said Jonathan. 'If we fall off this ledge. . .'

'Do you think you deserve to die?' repeated Mindius.

'Yes,' said Jonathan. 'And so do you.'

'You're right,' said Mindius. 'We both deserve to die.' He was silent for a moment and then added. 'But someone died for us. God sent his son as a sacrifice, that we might live.'

Jonathan gave a bitter smile at the irony of being preached the gospel by a criminal mastermind.

'You're Jewish, aren't you?' said Mindius.

Jonathan nodded.

'Then you know what a mikvah is: a ceremonial cleansing.'

'Yes.'

'A few days ago,' said Mindius, 'I underwent the ceremonial cleansing in the Little Maeander, at the hand of a prophet called Tychicus. A Jew, like us. Only he believes the Messiah has come. The Messiah – the Christ – was a man called Jesus, and he was the ultimate sacrifice. This Jesus taught a mikvah – a baptism – for the forgiveness of sins. You go down into the water and when you come up the old you is dead and there is a new you. One who can start fresh.'

Jonathan was silent. He knew this. How could he have forgotten it?

'Tychicus baptised me,' continued Mindius, 'and when I came up out of the water, I felt clean. And I remember thinking: *Now I can be good.*'

Don't believe him, said the voice. **He's a criminal mastermind**.

'The old me died three days ago. The new me is going to devote the rest of my life to doing good,' said Mindius. 'And you can, too. God's atoning sacrifice was so great. It means no crime is too big for him to forgive.'

Do you really believe that? said the voice.

'Yes,' said Jonathan quietly. 'I believe that.'

'Then accept his sacrifice,' urged Mindius, 'and be baptised. Die to your old self. Be born from above and become his servant. Live your life for good.'

Jonathan's head was throbbing. Mindius was a despicable monster. A criminal mastermind. But he was also Midas, the Key. Maybe this was the answer Jonathan had been seeking.

'Will you do that?' Mindius's voice seemed to be getting weaker.

Don't listen to him, said the voice.

'Will you be baptised?' whispered Mindius. 'Right here? Right now? In this pool of water?'

Jonathan took a deep breath and gave single nod. 'Yes,' he said.

There was a pause: 'I don't even know your name.'

'Jonathan ben Mordecai.'

'I have no authority,' said Mindius, 'except that given

to me by God through his Spirit. Are you sorry for what you've done?'

'More than I can say.'

'Then in the name of God the father, God the son and God the Holy Spirit, I baptise you, Jonathan ben Mordecai.'

SCROLL XXIII

'Jonathan?' came Flavia's voice from above. 'Are you alive?'

'I think so,' he said.

'Oh praise Juno! We thought you were dead!'

'Is Mindius with you?' came Bato's voice.

'Yes,' said Jonathan. 'I think he's unconscious. There's blood in the water and it's not mine.'

'We're going to lower a rope down,' said Bato. 'Tie it around him. We'll lift him up first, then drop it back to you.'

'Are you all right, Jonathan?' came Flavia's voice. 'Did Mindius hurt you?'

'No, he didn't hurt me,' said Jonathan. And he added quietly. 'I think he saved me.'

They spent the night at the house of an asiarch in Hierapolis. A doctor had set Mindius's broken leg and wrapped it in a splint. Now Mindius was sleeping in a room guarded by Bato and his two soldiers.

Jonathan had soaked for nearly half an hour in one of the thermal hot springs and the doctor had bound his sprained ankle. The asiarch's wife had given them cold chicken and bread for supper. Now Jonathan and Flavia were lying on soft felt mattresses on the flat roof of the house, lulled by the murmur of the water in the cascades below the city.

Jonathan gazed up at the myriad stars in the sky above. For the first time in years, maybe in his whole life, he felt free.

'Jonathan?' came Flavia's voice from the darkness beside him. 'Are you awake?'

'Yes,' he said.

'I feel so foolish,' said Flavia. 'We were chasing that baby and we never even had any proof it was Miriam's.'

'Miriam's baby disappeared at the same time as other children from Ostia,' said Jonathan. 'And most of them ended up here in Asia. Also, Magnus the dwarf told us it was Miriam's baby.'

'Only after we asked him why Mindius had kidnapped Popo. That probably gave him the idea to lie, to taunt us.'

'Yes,' agreed Jonathan. 'He probably just said that to get revenge on us.'

'He's a horrid, spiteful little dwarf,' said Flavia. 'I can't believe he tricked me.'

Jonathan sighed. 'It wasn't just you. We were all convinced it was Miriam's baby. Including your father and Bato. That's why they came to Asia.'

Flavia was silent for a few moments. Then she said: 'I miss home.'

'Me, too. What do you miss most?'

'Pater, of course. And Scuto and Alma and Caudex. And Alma's cooking. I never knew how lucky I was.'

'No,' agreed Jonathan. 'Neither did I.'

'What do you miss?'

'I miss father and mother,' he said. 'And Miriam. But

I miss them the way they used to be. And it will never be like that again.'

'Does that make you sad?'

'Yes. And no. Life goes on. It never goes back. We have to face the future.'

'That's very optimistic of you,' said Flavia, and he heard her yawn. 'You must be feeling better.'

'Yes.'

'Oh, look! A shooting star!'

'Yes,' said Jonathan. 'In the constellation of Virgo.'

For a moment they lay in silence, gazing up at the vast heavens. 'Jonathan,' said Flavia. 'Do you really think Mindius has turned good?'

'Yes, I do think Mindius has turned good. I think God is going to use him for great things.'

'I don't think god would use an evil man like that.'

'Moses and King David were both murderers,' said Jonathan. 'God used them.'

'Well, I don't think Mindius turned good. I think he's trying to trick us.'

Jonathan gazed up at the stars he knew so well and smiled. 'There's only one way to find out for certain.'

'What's that?'

'*By their fruit you will know them.* We'll just have to wait and see.'

In his vision he sees a man building a palace in heaven.

The man does this by giving his property to the poor. When he gives to widows and orphans he lays the foundations. Each coin in a beggar's palm buys a celestial brick. Every redeemed slave is a column for the peristyle. When he builds a nymphaeum for the town, his inner courtyard gains a fountain. And his alms to the synagogue build the roof.

The man has nothing left on earth.

All his treasure is stored up in heaven, and his mansion stands ready and waiting.

SCROLL XXIV

Bato assigned the blue-eyed soldier called Demetrius to accompany Jonathan and Flavia back to Ephesus. Jonathan's mare Tiberina seemed to sense a change in him, and she stepped out cheerfully, eating up the miles. The journey took three days. They spent both nights beside the Maeander River and when Jonathan awoke on the third morning to birdsong and sunlight, he realised what was different.

The voice had not spoken to him since the evening on the mountain. And he sensed he was free of it for ever.

As soon as Flavia saw Nubia and Aristo standing in the vestibule of the Villa Vinea, she knew something had happened.

'What is it?' said Flavia, looking from Nubia to Aristo and back. They stood side by side, both smiling. Their eyes had a strange shine. Nubia wore a beatific look on her face and Aristo looked almost boyish. 'Great Juno's peacock!' cried Flavia. 'You're betrothed!'

A look of utter astonishment flitted across Aristo's face.

Nubia's smile faded and her golden eyes grew wide. 'No!' she gasped, covering her mouth with her hand. 'It is not that.'

Aristo laughed. 'Of course not! It's something even better.'

Jonathan limped past Flavia into the courtyard. 'Is it Lupus? Has he been healed?'

'He still has no tongue,' said Nubia. 'But he has been healed inside. And we are born from above!'

Flavia opened her mouth, then closed it again.

Aristo beamed. 'A man called John has been staying with us. He's been telling us about The Way.'

'The way? What way?' said Flavia. 'What are you babbling about?'

'My faith!' cried Jonathan. 'You believe.'

'Yes!' cried Nubia. 'It is wonderful. And, Flavia, we do not have to sacrifice animals ever again.'

Jonathan limped forward to give her a hug, then turned to Aristo. 'You, too?'

Aristo nodded. 'I've had many conversations with your father about his philosophy. I always said I would believe it if I could see it. But old John said I wouldn't be able to see until I believed. He urged me to take the leap of faith.'

'Leap of faith?' said Flavia. 'It's not logical. Aristo, you taught me to use logic and reason. Flaccus says this religion is irrational. They believe without reasoning out their argument.'

'I taught you to use logic *and* imagination,' he said with a smile. 'Faith is a kind of imagination. It's imagining a world we can't see, but hope is there. When I prayed with John, a kind of veil was taken from my eyes. Flavia!' He took her excitedly by the shoulders. 'For the first time I understand the cosmos.' His eyes were shining.

'Lupus believes, too,' said Nubia. 'You should see him.'

'Where is he?' asked Jonathan, looking around happily.

'With the other children. And John and Ursus.'

'Ursus? Mindius's big thug of a bodyguard?'

'Yes,' Nubia giggled behind her hand. 'He is like a big toddler now.'

Jonathan began to laugh, too, and Flavia stared at the three of them.

'Great Juno's peacock,' she exclaimed. 'What's got into you all? You're all acting as if you've drunk too much wine.'

Bato arrived back in Ephesus two days later, three days after the Ides of August. He came into the palm tree courtyard shortly before noon as Flavia, Jonathan and Lupus were draping garlands from the columns.

'What's all this?' he said, raising an eyebrow at the sight of the garlands.

'Today is Nubia's birthday,' said Flavia. She was handing the end of a garland to Jonathan, who stood on a stool. 'She's thirteen.'

'We're having a special banquet at the tenth hour,' added Jonathan over his shoulder. He came carefully down from the stool, favouring his sore ankle.

'You're welcome to come!' added Flavia. 'If you like.'

'Where's the birthday girl?' Bato looked around. 'And where's Aristo?'

Lupus was also up on a stool. He grunted and pointed towards the Orpheus courtyard.

'Aristo has started teaching the children,' Flavia explained. 'He teaches them every morning. Nubia helps him; she looks after the younger ones.'

'What a good idea,' said Bato. 'Good for them.'

'Do you have any news for us?' asked Flavia.

Bato nodded. 'Baby Nicholas is very well. The waters of Hierapolis cured his rash. He and his mother Chloe are on their way back to Smyrna, to rejoin her family.'

'And Mindius?' asked Jonathan. 'Where is he?'

'In the basilica cells, I hope,' said Flavia. 'Awaiting trial.'

'Not exactly,' said Bato. 'I let him go.'

Lupus gave Bato his bug-eyed look and Flavia squealed: 'You let him go? You let Biggest Buyer go? The man we've been trying to catch for three years?'

Bato shrugged. 'Biggest Buyer as we know him is gone. The man I released has given away all his belongings. He has no possessions other than the tunic he wears and the sandals on his feet. And therefore, he has no power.'

'Of course he has power!' cried Flavia. 'He's probably just pretended to give his riches away. He's tricked you!'

Outside the walls of the villa, the gongs of Ephesus began to clang noon.

'Calm down,' said Bato, with his half smile. He took a scroll from his belt. 'I have a rather extraordinary document here. I'll show it to you as soon as Nubia arrives.'

Lupus grunted and pointed.

They turned to see Nubia coming into the courtyard with Xanthia and Euodia. Each of them was holding a kitten.

'Salve, Marcus Artorius Bato,' said Nubia politely.

'Salve, Nubia,' he replied. 'And Happy Birthday. I was just telling your friends I have some news for you. Will you sit?'

Flavia, Nubia and the two little girls sat on a cedar-wood bench in the shaded colonnade. Jonathan leaned against a column and Lupus pulled up a stool.

'Mindius was a very rich man,' said Bato. 'He owned three villas and several warehouses full of carpets. In this document he donates all the carpets to the guild here in Ephesus. It seems that Daphne's guild is not a collection of leather-workers, as I originally thought, but a congregation of those who follow The Way, your so-called Christians. He also says that I can claim two of the properties.'

'He's giving *you* two of his villas?' said Jonathan.

Flavia narrowed her eyes. 'That sounds a lot like a bribe,' she said. 'Like that townhouse in Ostia you got for testifying against us!'

Bato's face grew pink. 'It's not a bribe. I can only keep these villas providing I run them as a refuge for orphaned and sick children.'

'What about the third property?' asked Jonathan.

'He's giving that to the four of you. Under the same conditions.'

Flavia stared at Bato, open-mouthed. 'Us? He's giving one of his villas to us?'

'As long as you take in kidnapped and orphaned children, and feed the poor. He wants to use his wealth for good.'

'Which villa?' asked Jonathan. 'Which villa is he giving us?'

'Whichever one you want. There is one in Ostia, one in Halicarnassus and this one, here in Ephesus. You get first choice. I take over the remaining two. I should tell you,' he added. 'The Ostia property includes revenue from the salt fields, the Halicarnassus one has some olive groves and this villa has a good-sized vineyard on Mount Coressus, beyond the town walls.'

Lupus whistled in amazement.

'But how does Mindius know us?' said Nubia. 'I have never even seen him.'

'I told him about you,' said Bato. 'It was the least I could do after the um . . . court case last year. There's only one condition. None of you is of age yet, so the estate must be in an adult's name.'

'Aristo?' said Nubia.

'Or Marcus Flavius Geminus,' said Bato. 'I've sent messengers to Rhodes and Halicarnassus to let him know you're here in Ephesus.'

'Praise Juno!' cried Flavia, and added, 'I hope they reach him soon.'

'He should be here any day,' said Bato. 'In the meantime, do you have any idea which property you'd like to keep?'

'Ostia, of course,' said Flavia.

'If we aren't still wanted for treason,' said Jonathan.

'Oh! I forgot about that.'

'What about this one?' said Nubia softly. 'The Villa Vinea?'

'Yes! Stay!' cried Xanthia and Euodia together, hopping up and down on the padded seat of the bench.

'What about you, Lupus?' asked Jonathan. 'Where do you want to stay?'

Lupus thought for a moment, then wrote: IF WE CAN'T GO HOME TO OSTIA, I LIKE IT HERE.

SCROLL XXV

Nubia's birthday party had been a great success, with feasting and music and party games for all the children. It had continued even after sundown, and now it was the morning of the next day, the day some called the Lord's Day. In honour of Nubia's birthday, old John himself had come to take the service. Flavia imitated the posture of the others, with her face turned to the sky, her eyes closed tight and her hands lifted up. She was waiting for something to happen. Nubia said she had felt an intense heat from the top of her head to the soles of her feet. Aristo said it felt like being washed clean. Lupus was always smiling these days. And Jonathan had a new calmness and serenity.

But she felt nothing. Just a vague tingling in the palms of her hands.

Flavia opened one eye and looked around. Everyone seemed lost in worship. Even Lupus was making a joyful noise with his tongueless mouth. The children seemed happy, too. Sapphira's cheeks were wet but she had a smile on her face. Xanthia and Euodia were holding hands.

Flavia closed her eyes again and waited.

Nothing.

She opened her eyes again, sighed loudly and glanced

around. But nobody noticed, so she slipped out of the canal garden in the direction of the latrines, then hurried upstairs to her room. There, she put on her boy's tunic and tucked her hair up into her sunhat and took the front stairs down to the atrium. One of Bato's soldiers had been posted as a guard at the front door. He smiled and lifted the bolt and as the double doors closed behind her she heard it fall back into place.

Flavia stood for a moment, leaning against one of the columns of the porch and letting the early morning sun warm her face. She could hear the faint sound of her friends worshipping inside but now a new sound attracted her attention. A rhythmic, solemn blend of flutes, drums and cymbals drew her down to the street that cut across the careful street grid of the town, down the hill towards the harbour. She knew its name now: the Embolos.

When she reached it, she saw a procession of young priests and city officials passing by. They were carrying various statues of gold and silver, dazzling in the morning sun. She recognised a statue of Titus, and also one showing a young man spearing a boar. Flavia guessed it was Androclus, the young Athenian who had founded the city. As the last of the officials passed by, some members of the crowd moved into the street to join the procession.

Beside Flavia, a young woman holding a pink parasol turned to go back up towards the terraced houses.

'Excuse me,' said Flavia in her best Greek. 'What's happening?'

The woman smiled and replied, but her Greek was so heavily accented that Flavia only understood the words 'procession' and 'Artemis'.

'They're going to the Temple of Artemis?' asked Flavia.

'Yes,' said the young woman in her heavy accent. 'Coming and going.' She described a circle with her hand.

'Thank you,' said Flavia, and turned to gaze thoughtfully after the procession. She knew the great Temple of Artemis lay northeast of the city, a few miles outside the city walls. None of the others had wanted to visit the temple but she longed to see it. Why not now? She should be safe among the crowds and disguised as a boy.

She pulled down the brim of her sunhat and moved out to join the others following behind. At the bottom of the Embolos, the procession turned right onto Stadium Street, and passed slowly between shaded colonnades and splashing fountains. Flavia follow the procession past the massive Harbour Agora on her left and the theatre on her right, carved into Mount Pion. Its upper parts were covered in scaffolding. There were signs of renovation and building everywhere. Ephesus was a prosperous city, big and growing bigger.

Her heart beat faster as she passed the road which led down to the Market Basilica, where they had spent a night in the cells, but nobody was looking at her and presently she relaxed.

The procession turned right past the stadium and approached the Coressian Gate. At this point many Ephesians stopped and turned to go back to their places of work. But with a flourish of flutes and cymbals, the priests and musicians carried on out through the gate. After only a moment's hesitation, so did Flavia.

The road leading out of the city was lined with tall dark cypress trees, and with the tombs of the dead.

Behind the tombs were melon patches and peach orchards. Flavia stayed close behind a group of three women leading a goat. The musicians were still playing their strange rhythmic tune, and now Flavia could hear the priests chanting the name of Artemis. The sun blazed in the blue sky and a cool breeze ruffled her tunic. A bridge took them over a cheerful stream. Aristo had been teaching them about Ephesus, and Flavia knew it was only the brook called Marnas. The proper Cayster River was somewhere over to her left. And now the magnificent temple came into view up ahead, rising above the flat river plain. The sun gleamed on its red roof and painted columns.

She remembered a report she had once done for Aristo on the Seven Sights. According to Pliny's *Natural History*, the temple faced west, towards the sea. It contained a veritable forest of massive ionic columns – one hundred and twenty seven – some gilded and all of them carved.

The roadside tombs stopped abruptly at this point and she guessed they were entering the temenos, the sacred precinct around the temple.

As she approached the temple, she thought of Flaccus.

'Oh, Floppy,' she whispered. 'I wish you were here with me. The Temple of Artemis is one of the Seven Sights and I know you wanted to see it.'

Suddenly a thought occurred to her. Ephesus was not far from Halicarnassus, only two days by road. What if he had come to see the Temple? What if he was here now? Alone?

Without Prudentilla by his side he would confess that he really loved Flavia and that he had only settled for someone else because he thought she was dead. He would agree to break his engagement to Prudentilla at once. Then he would take Flavia in his arms and kiss her and in a few years they would marry and their life together would be sublimely happy.

Flavia passed the three women and their goat; they had turned to go up the steps of a large colonnaded structure; she knew it must contain the altar, for the Temple itself lay beyond. The goat bleated plaintively, as if it sensed its fate.

The tail end of the procession was just disappearing inside and for a moment she stood, letting her head tip back as she took in the grandeur of the monument filling the sky above her. Slowly she mounted the marble steps and entered the forest of massive columns. The air between them was clouded with incense and the smell of it made her dizzy. From somewhere in the inner reaches came the faint sound of the flute and drums, no longer moving. The procession had found its destination.

She could not enter the cella – it was filled with musicians, priests and statues – but she stopped to look at some of the smaller cult statues of the goddess outside. One in particular made her stare in amazement.

This brightly painted statue showed the goddess wearing a tall hat, like a decorated beehive, and a floor-length robe covered with carved animals, including the signs of the Zodiac. Strangest of all, the goddess seemed to have two dozen breasts. Flavia wrinkled her nose in distaste; this Asian Artemis did not bear any resemblance to the proper Roman Diana.

The thought of Diana reminded Flavia of the vow she had made nine months before: a vow to remain a virgin for her whole life and never marry. Maybe Diana was punishing her for going back on that vow. Maybe Diana was angry that she wanted to marry Flaccus.

Suddenly Flavia had an idea: she would make Aristo's leap of faith and test Jonathan's god. If he could heal the sick and bring people back from the dead, he could certainly do one little thing for her.

Heart pounding, Flavia closed her eyes and prayed. 'Dear god of Jonathan, if you are really powerful enough to raise a man from the dead, please make Flaccus be here right now, and make him love me.'

She concentrated very hard, and with her eyes closed, she could easily visualise him: his glossy dark hair and long-lashed dark eyes, his white teeth and smooth tanned skin. She knew his lips would taste like mastic and be very soft. She opened her eyes, and looked around expectantly, her heart pounding.

Perhaps he would appear from behind this very statue and take her in his arms.

But he didn't, and although she wandered among the massive columns for almost an hour, she couldn't find him.

And when she got back to the villa, over two hours after she had left, her friends were still singing and praising.

They hadn't even noticed her absence.

In his vision he sees a celestial battle.

The sky is cobalt blue and full of stars. The whole of the Zodiac is there, as if inked in light on the inside of a vast bowl. Virgo. Leo. Aquarius. Stars pursue and confront each other with terrible purpose across this apocalyptic background.

Then he sees something new.

Against a backdrop of dying stars, two brothers are

struggling. Like Jacob and Esau. Castor and Pollux. Romulus and Remus. Dark against Light. Good against Evil. Ice against Fire.

A crescent moon – blood red and unimaginably huge –sinks in the west. And in the east a comet appears, its tail flaming, destroying stars as it goes.

Jonathan woke with a gasp, the images from his dream fresh in his mind. For the first time, he understood the meaning.

'It's not about Flavia,' he whispered. 'It's about Titus and Domitian. The oracle said that whoever possessed "Nero's Eye" would rule Rome. *That* is its real value. Domitian wanted it for himself because he wants to be emperor.'

He sat up and looked at the dim wall opposite, flickering in the light of a tiny oil-lamp.

'What if Titus's headaches aren't what they seem?' he said to himself. 'What if Domitian is slowly poisoning him?'

Jonathan pulled back the sheet and quietly rose to his feet. The dim night-light showed Lupus fast asleep on his own bed. His legs were tangled in a sheet, but his face looked calm and at peace. Jonathan glanced up at the small high window. Beyond the iron grille, the sky was black, but somewhere in the distance a cock was crowing. He guessed it was still a few hours until dawn.

He looked back down at Lupus. 'I wish you could come with me,' he whispered to his sleeping friend. 'But it's too dangerous. And this is part of my new life.'

Quietly he took Lupus's wax tablet from the bedside table, and he began to write.

SCROLL XXVI

Someone was poking Flavia.

'Mmmph!' she said. 'What is it?' She turned over to see who was prodding her.

'Lupus!' she muttered. 'Go back to sleep. It's still night.'

Lupus left her and she rolled over and snuggled her head into the pillow. Then she heard Lupus grunting and Nubia's voice asking, 'What is wrong?'

Flavia groaned and sat up. Nubia was holding Lupus's wax tablet up to the little night oil-lamp.

After a moment she looked up at Flavia, her eyes dark gold in the dim light. 'It is Jonathan,' she said. 'He is gone.'

Jonathan ben Mordecai, to his friends Flavia, Nubia and Lupus, and to his tutor Aristo.

By the time you read this I will be gone. Don't be upset that I didn't say goodbye. You probably would have tried to convince me not to go. And you might have succeeded. But this is something I have to do.

For the past few weeks I have been having dreams. Or visions. I'm not sure what they are. I only know they have been getting stronger and stronger, especially a dream of a spiritual battle in the constellation of Gemini. I have had this dream several times. Tonight I had it again and I finally think I know what it means: Titus is in danger from his brother Domitian.

Once I tried to kill Titus. Now I have a chance to make it right and I think God is calling me to do this. I am going to go to Rome to warn Titus and to help if I can. Please don't follow me. It will be very dangerous. If I reach Titus I will try to explain about the warrant for our arrest and get him to revoke it. Then you will be able to come home again.

In the meantime, stay in Ephesus, so that I will know where to find you.

I pray that you will all stay happy and healthy and that one day I will see you again. Shalom.

P.S. I don't hear the voice anymore.

P.P.S. Erase this message once you have read it.

Nubia patted Flavia on the back. Her friend was weeping.

'I can't believe it,' sobbed Flavia. 'He's gone without us. How could he do that? We're a team! The old Jonathan wouldn't have done that.'

'He does not want to endanger us,' said Nubia softly.

'But now Jonathan will be in danger!'

'What can we do?' said a voice from the door. Nubia looked up to see Aristo, looking tousled and handsome in the lamplight.

'We cannot go with him,' said Nubia. 'We are needed here.'

'Also, if we went with him to Rome then the three of you would risk being arrested,' said Aristo.

'But so will he!' cried Flavia.

'Then let's stop him!' said Aristo. 'Someone else can

warn Titus. Someone who isn't wanted or known to the authorities. Someone like me.'

Lupus grunted and pointed at Aristo, as if to say: *He's right*.

'Come on then!' cried Flavia, wiping away her tears and slipping on her sandals.

'Where?' asked Nubia.

'To the harbour!' said Flavia. 'If Jonathan's going to Rome then he'll be going by boat.'

Nubia nodded and rose and as she slipped on her sandals she wished there was something she could do. Then she remembered there was. She closed her eyes and silently prayed: 'Lord, please protect and guide Jonathan. Amen.'

Flavia, Nubia, Lupus and Aristo ran down Harbour Street. Although it was getting light in the east, the torches were still burning in the wall brackets, and shopkeepers were only just raising their shutters.

The docks were busy, however. Night fishermen were bringing in their catches, stevedores were rolling barrels and carrying amphoras, and the customs officials had already set up their tables.

Flavia and her friends stopped and looked around, still panting from the exertion of their run.

'Do you see him?' cried Flavia.

'No,' said Aristo.

'Behold!' cried Nubia, and then said. 'No, it is not Jonathan.'

A tall young sailor with green eyes was announcing the imminent departure of the merchant ship *Fortuna*, bound for Alexandria.

Flavia ran forward to ask him if he'd taken on any

curly-haired passengers, but as she reached him, her view of the water was unobstructed and for the first time she noticed two ships coming into dock and one moving out into the canal.

'What ship is that?' Flavia asked the sailor. 'The one leaving.' He turned and squinted in the direction she was pointing.

'*Helpis*, I think. Captained by Zenon.'

'Where's it going?' panted Aristo, who had caught up to Flavia. 'Do you know?'

'Ostia,' said Green Eyes. 'She's bound for the port of Ostia.'

'Oh no!' cried Flavia. 'We're too late.'

Flavia sat on a coil of rope and put her head in her hands.

Emotions from the past half year swept over her. Her refusal of Floppy's proposal in March had caused the argument with her father, which had made her accept the emperor's mission. And that had resulted in months away from home, facing danger and even death in strange lands. Over these past months her friends had been with her. But now Jonathan was gone, Nubia, Aristo and Lupus had converted to a strange religion, and Floppy was engaged to someone else.

Nubia was patting her back but it didn't help. She had never felt so alone.

Flavia wept.

Suddenly there was a familiar panting and the smell of doggy breath, and a hot wet tongue was lathering her face.

Flavia opened her eyes in disbelief. 'Scuto?' she whispered. And then: 'Scuto!' She threw her arms around the woolly neck of her beloved dog.

'Flavia?' called a familiar voice. 'Flavia. Is that you?'

Flavia jumped up and squealed with delight. 'Pater!' she cried. 'Oh, pater! You found us!'

He was pushing his way through the sailors, looking older and thinner but now his arms were around her and she was safe in his embrace. 'Flavia,' he cried. 'Praise the gods!'

'Oh pater!' she said again, and burst into tears.

Nubia was in tears, too, for her dog Nipur was there. So was the Geminus family door-slave, Caudex. He stood waiting shyly with the Captain's bags. Flavia hugged Caudex and then Nipur, and then her father again. When everyone had greeted one another, they started walking slowly back up Harbour Street.

As they passed shops and fountains, the two dogs ran back and forth with their noses down in a delirium of excitement at the smells of Ephesus. Every so often they would rush back to their mistresses and pant happily up at them.

'Pater, I can't believe you brought Scuto. You always said having a dog on board a ship is bad luck.'

'He reminded me of you, my little owl,' said her father, and kissed the top of her straw hat.

Lupus grunted and pointed at Nipur.

Flavia's father smiled. 'Nipur refused to be parted from Scuto.'

'My cup of joy is overflowing,' said Nubia, her face radiant.

'Pater,' said Flavia, 'it wasn't Popo that Mindius took. It was another baby. And Jonathan's gone to Rome to see Titus, even though there's a warrant for our arrest. Your ship probably passed his in the harbour.'

Captain Geminus shook his head in wonder. 'I still can't believe you're alive,' he said. 'I thought you were all drowned.' He made the sign against evil. 'What brought you to Asia?'

'Aristo,' explained Nubia. 'He brought us to Asia because you were here.'

'I found them in Alexandria,' said Aristo, 'after some er . . . notices were posted in Ostia.'

'Yes,' said Flavia breathlessly. 'Our ship home from Mauretania was blown off course and ran aground off the coast of Egypt. We went all the way up the Nile and then back again – I'll tell you later – and then we found out we were wanted, so we couldn't leave. Last week Aristo found us and told us that you were looking for Popo in Halicarnassus, so we went there. And then we followed Mindius here to Ephesus because we thought he had Popo but we were wrong. It wasn't him.'

'I know,' said her father. 'I mean, I know about Popo. That he wasn't one of the children brought here to Asia.'

'How?' cried Flavia. 'We only just found out.'

He stopped and turned to look at her, so the others stopped, too.

'Two days ago,' said Captain Geminus, 'I received a letter from Jonathan's mother. The boy who claimed he saw Rhodian slavers take Lydia and Popo from the market later confessed he was lying. Someone bribed him to say that.'

'Who?'

'Lydia.'

'What?' cried Flavia and Aristo together.

And Nubia said: 'Lydia the wet-nurse?'

Captain Geminus nodded grimly. 'Jonathan's mother thinks Lydia was mourning the loss of her own baby and wanted Popo for her own. We don't know where she's taken him. It could be anywhere in the Empire.'

'Oh, no!' cried Flavia.

'Don't fret, little owl,' said her father, picking up his satchel and starting to walk again. 'We'll find him. And Jonathan, too. In the meantime I hear you've been helping Bato with the kidnapped children here in Ephesus?'

'That's right,' said Aristo. 'Mindius had a villa full of illegal slaves, all children. Some were working in a carpet factory; others were being groomed as ... personal slaves. We've reunited some of them with their families, but there are still more than three dozen left.'

'Pater, one of them is Sapphira, who disappeared from Ostia three years ago!'

Aristo added, 'Apparently Mindius has renounced his evil ways and left his property to Bato.'

Lupus grunted, then pointed at himself and the others.

Flavia interpreted: 'And to us!'

Captain Geminus ruffled Lupus's hair and slipped his free arm around Flavia's shoulder. 'I don't understand half of what you're saying,' he laughed. 'All I know is that you're alive and well. I suppose I'll have to sacrifice an entire sheep as a thanks offering.'

'No,' said Nubia and Aristo, while Lupus tipped his head back in the Greek gesture for no.

'What?'

'No more animal sacrifices,' said Nubia with a radiant smile. 'Never again.'

'What in Hades are you talking about?'

'I'll explain it to you later,' said Aristo.

'Don't listen to them, pater,' said Flavia happily. 'I

think it's just a phase they're going through. They've all gone a bit mad for Jonathan's religion. For some reason they think there's no more need for sacrifices.'

Ten days later, on the Kalends of September, the merchant ship *Helpis* docked at Ostia.

A dark-eyed boy in a wide-brimmed straw travelling hat came off the gangplank and stood looking around for a few moments. He had a hemp shoulder bag over one arm but no other luggage.

'Name?' said an official with a wax tablet.

'Adam,' said the youth in Greek. 'A Jew from Alexandria. On my way to Rome to study engineering.'

'Any goods you want to declare?' said the man.

'All my possessions are on me,' said the boy, turning his palms up.

The official looked him up and down, taking in the cheap but sturdy sandals, the long-sleeved tunic and the wide-brimmed hat.

'Got any money?'

'I have fifty sesterces.' The boy touched the leather coin pouch at his belt. 'And a letter of recommendation addressed to a Jew named Josephus at the Imperial court.' The boy opened his shoulder bag. 'Do you want to see it?'

The official glanced in the bag. He could see a folded cloak, a bath set and a sealed wax tablet. 'Not really,' he said. 'Just pay the usual two sesterces harbour tax and you're on your way.'

The youth nodded, slung his bag back over his shoulder and fished in the coin purse. A moment later he handed over two bronze coins.

'Very well,' said the official, and waved him on.

The boy made his way through the noisy dockyards to the Marina Gate and passed beneath its shaded arch. He took a long drink of cool water at the marina fountain and bought some figs from a street vendor near the fish market. At the crossroads he turned right along the Decumanus Maximus and made his way to the town forum, where he paused to read the previous day's acta diurna on the noticeboard. When he read the notice offering a reward for a Jewish boy named Jonathan, two girls and a mute boy, he glanced around.

Pulling down the brim of his hat, he continued on down the Decumanus Maximus, passing the theatre on his left and red-brick granaries on his right. When he reached the turning for Green Fountain Street, he resisted the temptation to look right towards his old home. His eyes resolutely ahead, he passed through the Roman Gate, along the tomb-lined Via Ostiensis towards Rome, the Eternal City.

One step at a time, Jonathan moved towards his destiny.

ARISTO'S SCROLL

Acta diurna (*ak*-ta die-*urn*-uh)
(lit. 'actions of the day') announcements of births, marriages, deaths, decrees and other news posted daily on a board in the forum of Rome and probably Ostia, too

Aegean (uh-*jee*-un)
sea between modern Greece and Asia Minor (Turkey)

agora (ag-o-*rah*)
the Greek equivalent of the Latin forum, an open space for markets and meetings

Alexandria (al-ex-*an*-dree-uh)
Egypt's great port, at the mouth of the Nile Delta founded by and named after Alexander the Great; in the first century AD it was second only to Rome in wealth, fame and importance

amphitheatre (*am*-fee-theatre)
an oval-shaped stadium for watching gladiator shows, beast fights and the execution of criminals

amphora (*am*-for-uh)
large clay storage jar for holding wine, oil, grain, etc.

Androclus (an-dro-kluss)
son of the Athenian king Codrus, an Ionian; he founded Ephesus

apocalyptic (a-pok-a-*lip*-tik)

having to do with the Apocalypse (Greek for 're-velation') the final destruction of the world at the end of time

Apollo (uh-*pol*-oh)

god of music, disease and healing

Aquarius (a-*kwar*-ee-uss)

sign of the Zodiac of the water-carrier

aqueduct (*ak*-wa-dukt)

man-made channel for carrying water, they had tall arches when carrying water across a valley or plain

Arabia (uh-*ray*-bee-uh)

in Roman times land on the right bank of the Nile, (to the east) was considered Arabia

Aramaic (air-uh-*may*-ik)

closely related to Hebrew, it was the common language of first century Jews

Artemis (*art*-a-miss)

Greek goddess of the hunt (and fertility in Asia Minor) and Apollo's twin sister; often identified with Roman Diana; Ephesus was an important centre of her cult

Artemisia (art-uh-*mee*-zyah)

wife of Mausolus of Caria; after his death she drank his ashes, then had a magnificent tomb construced for him: one of the Seven Sights of the ancient world

Asia (*azhe*-ya)

in Roman times, Asia was a province which is now part of modern Turkey; it was a senatorial province governed by a proconsul

asiarch (*azhe*-ee-ark)

Greek for 'ruler in Asia'; a kind of Roman official in the province of Asia

Athens (*ath*-inz)

(modern capital of Greece) in Roman times a university town devoted to the goddess of wisdom, Athena

atrium (*eh*-tree-um)

the reception room in larger Roman homes, often with skylight and pool

ballista (buh-*list*-uh)

catapult used in ancient times for hurling large stones

basilica (ba-*sill*-ik-uh)

large public building in most Roman towns; it served as a court of law and meeting place; there were often cells for holding prisoners until trial

caldarium (kal-*dar*-ee-um)

the hot room of the baths, often with steaming basins and underfloor heating

Calliope (kal-*eye*-oh-pee)

one of the nine muses from Greek mythology; her specialty was epic poetry

Canopus (kan-*oh*-puss)

town to the east of Alexandria on the Nile Delta; it was a famous Roman resort in the first century AD

Caria (*kare*-ee-ah)

ancient region of Turkey south of the Meander River and northwest of Lycia

carruca (kuh-*roo*-kuh)

a four-wheeled travelling carriage, usually mule-drawn and often covered

Castor (*kas*-tor)

one of the famous twins of Greek mythology (Pollux being the other)

Catullus (ka-*tul*-uss)

Gaius Valerius Catullus (c.84–54 BC) was one of Rome's most famous poets

caupona (kow-*po*-na)

inn, tavern or shop, usually the former

Cayster (*kay*-stir)

Also known as the Little Maeander, this river flowed into the sea near the harbour of Ephesus

cella (*sell*-uh)

inner room of a temple; it usually housed the cult statue

ceramic (sir-*am*-ik)

clay which has been fired in a kiln, very hard and smooth

Cibotus (kib-*oh*-tuss)

Greek for 'box'; name of the man-made harbour which was part of Alexandria's larger western harbour

Cnidos (k'*nee*-doss)

famous town with a double harbour on a promontory in Asia Minor (Turkey)

colonnade (kal-uh-*nayd*)

a covered walkway lined with columns at regular intervals

Colossus of Rhodes (kuh-*loss*-iss)

gigantic statue of the sun god Helios on the island of Rhodes; considered one of the Seven Sights in the first century, even though it had fallen down by then

Coressian Gate

the northern gate of ancient Ephesus, despite the fact that Mount Coressus lies to the south

Coressus (kor-*ess*-uss)

Mount Coressus forms the southern slopes of the city of Ephesus

Decumanus Maximus (deck-yoo-*man*-uss *max*-ee-mus)
one of the two main streets of most Roman towns, the other being the 'cardo'

Demeter (d'-*mee*-tur)
Greek goddess of grain and the harvest; her daughter was Persephone

detectrix (dee-tek-tricks)
female form of 'detective' from Latin 'detego' – 'I uncover'

Domitian (duh-*mish*-un)
younger son of Vespasian; emperor Titus's younger brother by ten years, he is about thirty-one years old when this story takes place

Embolos (*em*-bo-loce)
Greek for 'wedge'; name of the famous paved road in Ephesus that angled down from the upper town towards the harbour

encaustic (en-*kow*-stik)
kind of painting done with hot or warm coloured wax, usually on hardwood

Endymion (en-*dim*-ee-on)
mythical youth of such beauty that Selene the moon goddess fell in love with him; Zeus put him into a perpetual sleep and gave him eternal youth so that Selene could always gaze upon him

Ephesus (*eff*-uh-siss)
perhaps the most important town in the Roman province of Asia and site of one of the Seven Wonders of the Ancient World, the Temple of Artemis

Etesian (ee-*tee*-zhyun)
Greek for 'yearly': the name of a strong dry north-westerly trade wind which blew in the summer across the Mediterranean

euge! (*oh*-gay)

Latin exclamation: 'hurray!'

eunuch (*yoo*-nuk)

a boy or man whose physical development has been halted by castration

Euromus (yur-*oh*-muss)

ancient town in Caria about half way between Halicarnassus and Ephesus; was famous for its Temple of Zeus

fenugreek (*fen*-yoo-greek)

from Latin faenum (hay) and Graecum (Greek); a white-flowered pea plant used as animal fodder in Roman times

Flaccus (*flak*-uss)

Gaius Valerius Flaccus, poet who began a Latin version of the *Argonautica* around AD 80

Flavia (*flay*-vee-a)

a name, meaning 'fair-haired'; Flavius is another form of this name

Flavian (*flay*-vee-un)

relating to the period of the three emperors Vespasian, Titus and Domitian: AD 69–96

forum (*for*-um)

ancient marketplace and civic centre in Roman towns

frigidarium (frig-id-*dar*-ee-um)

the cold plunge in Roman baths

Furies (*fyoo*-reez)

also known as the 'Kindly Ones', these mythical creatures looked like women with snaky hair; they tormented people guilty of terrible crimes

garum (*gar*-um)

very popular pungent sauce made of fermented fish parts, not unlike modern Worcestershire sauce

Gehenna (g'-*hen*-uh)

the place near Jerusalem where rubbish was burned; in Biblical writings it came to represent the place where evil is destroyed, i.e. 'hell'

Gemini (jem-in-ee)

Latin for 'twins'; often refers to the mythological twins Castor and Pollux or to their constellation in the night sky or to someone born under this sign

gladiator

man trained to fight other men in the arena, sometimes to the death

gustatio (goo-*stat*-yo)

first course or 'starter' of a Roman banquet; the main course was called *prima mensa*, 'the first table', and dessert was called *secunda mensa*, 'the second table'

Hades (*hay*-deez)

the Underworld, the place where the spirits of the dead were believed to go

Halicarnassus (hal-ee-car-*nass*-uss)

(modern Bodrum) ancient city in the region of Caria (now part of Turkey)

helpis (*hel*-piss)

Greek for 'hope'

Heracleia (h'-*rak*-lay-uh)

Ancient port on the southern slopes of Mount Latmus in Caria; Endymion was said to have slept in the caves above it

Hercules (*her*-kyoo-leez)

very popular Roman demi-god, the equivalent of Greek Herakles

Herodotus (huh-rod-a-tuss)

(c.484–425 BC) Greek historian from Halicarnassus; he was called 'the Father of History' because he was one of the first to collect material systematically

Hierapolis (hee-air-*rap*-oh-liss)
ancient city built above the amazing mineral cascades of modern Pamukkale; the disciple Philip is said to have been martyred there in AD 80

hospitium (hoss-*pit*-ee-um)
Latin for 'hotel' or 'guesthouse'; often very luxurious with baths and dining rooms

icterus (*ik*-tur-uss)
from Greek ikteros: the Latin word for jaundice, a disease that makes the skin and eyes appear yellow

Ides (eyedz)
thirteenth day of most months in the Roman calendar (including August); in March, May, July and October the Ides occur on the fifteenth day of the month

impluvium (im-*ploo*-vee-um)
a rectangular rainwater pool under a skylight (compluvium) in the atrium

insula (*in*-soo-la)
lit. 'island' but also the common word for a city block in Roman times

Ioannes (yo-*ah*-naze)
Greek for 'John'

Ionia (eye-*oh*-nee-uh)
ancient region of Turkey on the Aegean coast around Izmir (ancient Smyrna)

Ionian (eye-*oh*-nee-un)
member of an ancient Hellenic people from the region around Athens; they colonized part of Asia which became known as 'Ionia'

Ionic (eye-*on*-ik)
an order of architecture with columns whose capitals look like scrolls

Italia (it-*al*-ya)

the Latin word for Italy

Jerusalem (j'-*roo*-sa-lem)

capital city of Judea, until AD 70, when it was ransacked and destroyed by Roman legions commanded by Titus

Jesus AKA **Jesus Christ**

(C.3 BC–C.AD 30); Jewish carpenter and teacher who became the central figure of the Christian faith; his followers considered him to be the Christ or Messiah ('anointed one') and also the Son of God who was resurrected from the dead

Josephus (jo-*see*-fuss)

(AD 37–C.100) a Jewish commander during the famous Jewish revolt of AD 65; he surrendered to Vespasian, became Titus's freedman and lived in Rome, writing histories and other works, particularly about the Jews of that time

Juno (*joo*-no)

queen of the Roman gods and wife of the god Jupiter

Jupiter (*joo*-pit-er)

king of the Roman gods, husband of Juno and brother of Pluto and Neptune

Kalends (*kal*-ends)

the first day of any month in the Roman calendar

Laodicea (lay-oh-*diss*-yuh)

town a few miles below Hierapolis, by the time the hot waters from Hierapolis reached Laodicea, they were lukewarm; it had one of the seven churches mentioned in the Book of Revelation

lararium (lar-*ar*-ee-um)

household shrine, often a chest with a miniature temple on top, sometimes a niche

Latmus (lat-muss)

dramatically rocky ridge which used to be on the coast of Caria in Ionia; because of silting it is now inland, on the shore of Lake Bafa in southwest Turkey

Leo (*lee*-oh)

sign of the Zodiac of the lion

Lucifer (*loo*-s'-fur)

Latin for 'bringer of light'; a name for the morning star and also for Satan

Lydia (*lid*-ee-uh)

ancient region in Turkey north of Caria; its last king was Croesus

Lysimachus (lie-*sim*-a-kuss)

(c.355–281 BC) one of the successors of Alexander the Great; he rebuilt the defensive walls of Ephesus in the third century BC

Maeander (mee-*and*-ur)

ancient name for the Menderes, a river in Turkey which winds sinuously back and forth on its way to the sea; we get the word 'meander' from this river

Magnesia (aka Magnesia on the Meander)

ancient town on the Maeander River a few miles southeast of Ephesus, northwest of the present town of Magnesia

Magnesian Gate three-arched southeastern gate of Ephesus, leading to Magnesia and beyond

maquis (mak-*ee*)

French word for the dense and fragrant green scrub vegetation found in regions all over the Mediterranean, especially those near the coast

Marnas (*mar*-nass)

brook which provided one of the major water supplies for the city of Ephesus

Mauretania (more-uh-*tane*-ya)

(modern Morocco) one of the North African provinces of the Roman Empire

Mausoleum (maw-zo-*lee*-um)

The Mausoleum of Mausolus at Halicarnassus was one of the 'Seven Sights' of the ancient world; it was a giant tomb to a ruler named Mausolus, who lived in the fourth century BC; we get the word 'mausoleum' from the tomb named after him

Messiah (m'-*sigh*-uh)

Hebrew for 'anointed' or 'chosen' one; the Greek word is 'Christ'

metanoia (met-an-*oy*-uh)

lit. 'change of mind', the Greek word is often translated as 'repentance'

Midas (*my*-duss)

mythical king of Phrygia with several legends attached to him; in one, everything he touches turns to gold; in another, he gets ears like a satyr

mikvah (*mik*-vuh)

Hebrew for 'collection' (usually of waters); a bath in which Jewish ritual purifications were performed

Mindius (*min*-dee-uss)

name of a Jewish benefactor of the synagogue of Ostia

mite (might)

tiny bronze coin; the smallest denomination possible

Moriah (AKA Mount Moriah)

mountain upon which Abraham nearly sacrificed his son Isaac, according to the account in Genesis 22

Mount Latmus (*lat*-muss)

dramatically rocky ridge which used to be on the coast of Caria in Ionia; because of silting it is now inland, on the shore of Lake Bafa in southwest Turkey

Myndus (*min*-duss)

   Ancient Greek city in Caria on the coast a few miles
   west of Halicarnassus

Naucratis (now-*kra*-tiss)

   important Roman town on the Canopic branch of the
   Nile in the Nile Delta

Neptune (*nep*-tyoon)

   god of the sea; his Greek equivalent is Poseidon

Nero (*neer*-oh)

   Emperor who ruled Rome from AD 54–68

Nisyrus (*niss*-ee-russ)

   small, round volcanic island near the coast of Asia
   Minor (Turkey)

Nones (nonz)

   seventh day of March, May, July, October; fifth day of
   all the other months, including August

nymphaeum (nim-*fay*-um)

   a monument consecrated to the nymphs, most
   usually a fountain; therefore nymphaeum became a
   synonym for 'fountain'

odi et amo (*oh*-dee et *ah*-mo)

   'I hate and I love'; first line of a famous poem by
   Catullus

Ombos (*om*-boss)

   (modern Kom Ombo) town on the east bank of the
   Nile in Egypt

Orpheus (*or*-fee-uss)

   mythological lyre-player who charmed men, animals
   and rocks with his music, and who tried to bring back
   his wife from the land of the dead

oscilla (*ah*-sill-uh)

   Latin for 'little faces'; these were discs of marble,

wood or clay hung from trees or between columns to keep away birds and bad luck

Ostia (*oss*-tee-uh)
port about sixteen miles southwest of Rome; Ostia is Flavia's home town

Ourania (oo-*ran*-yuh)
Greek spelling of Urania, one of the nine muses, her discipline was astronomy

palla (*pal*-uh)
a woman's cloak, could also be wrapped round the waist or worn over the head

pantomime (*pan*-toe-mime)
Roman theatrical performance in which a man (or sometimes woman) illustrated a sung story through dance; the dancer could also be called a 'pantomime'

papyrus (puh-*pie*-russ)
papery material made of pounded Egyptian reeds, used as writing paper and also for parasols and fans

pater (*pa*-tare)
Latin for 'father'

patrician (pa-*trish*-un)
a person from the highest Roman social class

Paul of Tarsus
AKA St Paul, an early Christian who took the gospel to Greece and Asia; he lived in Ephesus for at least two years around AD 50

peristyle (*perry*-style)
a columned walkway around an inner garden or courtyard

Persephone (purr-*sef*-uh-nee)
beautiful young daughter of Demeter, she was abducted by Pluto while gathering flowers and had to spend six months of the year in the underworld

Pharos (*far*-oss)

name of an island off the coast of Alexandria on which a massive lighthouse was built; for this reason, people began to call the lighthouse 'pharos' too

Philadelphus (fill-a-*del*-fuss)

Lit. 'loves his brother'; popular male name in the Greek-speaking parts of the Roman empire

Phoenician (fuh-neesh-un)

Semitic sea-people who established trading posts in coastal positions all over the Mediterranean; they were renowned sailors

Phrygia (*frij*-ee-uh)

Part of Asia Minor (modern Turkey) to the east of Caria and Ionia; it was also sometimes used for the whole province of Asia

Pion (*pee*-on)

one of the mountains upon which Ephesus was built, also the name of the god of that mountain

Pliny (*plin*-ee)

(AD 23–79) Gaius Plinius Secundus was a famous Roman admiral and scholar who died in the eruption of Vesuvius in AD 79; his *Natural History* still survives

Pluto (*ploo*-toe)

Roman god of the underworld; his Greek equivalent is Hades

Pollux (*pol*-luks)

one of the famous twins of Greek mythology (Castor being the other)

posca (*poss*-kuh)

well-watered vinegar; a non-alcoholic drink particularly favoured by soldiers on duty

prima mensa (*pree*-ma *men*-sa)

Latin for 'the first table' or main course of a meal,

the starter was called *gustatio*; and dessert was called *secunda mensa*, 'the second table'

province (*pra*-vince)

a division of the Roman Empire; in the first century AD senatorial provinces were governed by a proconsul appointed by the senate, imperial provinces were governed by a propraetor appointed by the Emperor

quadrans (*kwad*-ranz)

tiny bronze coin worth one sixteenth of a sestertius or quarter of an as (hence quadrans); in the first century it was the lowest value Roman coin in production

Rhakotis (rah-*ko*-tiss)

western suburb of Alexandria; may have been the original fishing settlement

Rhodes (roads)

large island in the Aegean Sea near Turkey, its capital was Rhodes Town

Sabratha (sah-*brah*-tah)

(modern Tripoli Vecchia / Zouagha) one of the 'three cities' of Tripolitania in the North African province of Africa Proconsularis (now northern Libya)

satyr (*sat*-tur)

mythical woodland creature which is half man, half animal; in Roman times they were shown with goat's ears, tail, legs and horns

scroll (skrole)

a papyrus or parchment 'book', unrolled from side to side as it was read

secunda mensa (sek-*oon*-da *men*-sa)

Latin for 'the second table' or dessert course of a meal, the starter was called *gustatio*; and the main course was called *prima mensa*, 'the first table'

Selene (sel-*ee*-nee)

titaness who drove the chariot of the moon; she loved Endymion and Zeus put him in a perpetual sleep so that she could gaze upon him at night

Seneca (*sen*-eh-kuh)

(c.4 BC–AD 65) Roman philosopher who wrote about how to die a good death

sesterces (sess-*tur*-seez)

more than one sestertius, a brass coin; about a day's wage for a labourer

Smyrna (*smeer*-nuh)

(modern Izmir) ancient port city in Ionia, one of the seven churches mentioned in the Book of Revelation was located here

Soter (*so*-tare)

Lit. 'saviour'; popular male name in the Greek-speaking parts of the Roman empire

sponsa (spon-suh)

Latin for fiancée, wife or betrothed

stola (*stole*-uh)

a long sleeveless tunic worn mostly by Roman matrons (married women)

stylus (*stile*-us)

a metal, wood or ivory tool for writing on wax tablets

suppressio (suh-press-ee-oh)

Latin legal term for the abduction and enslavement of a person who is freeborn

Surrentum (sir-*wren*-tum)

modern Sorrento, a pretty harbour town on the Bay of Naples south of Vesuvius

Symi (*sim*-ee)

small island near Rhodes famous for its sponge-divers

tablinum (tab-*leen*-um)

room in wealthier Roman houses used as the master's study or office, often looking out onto the atrium or inner garden, or both

Tarquin (*tar*-kwin)

one of the first kings of Rome; lived in the sixth century BC

temenos (*tem*-en-oss)

sacred marked-out area, usually in a sanctuary

tesserae (*tess*-sir-eye)

the little cubes of stone and glass that make up a mosaic

tetradrachm (tet-ra-*drak*-m)

coin of the Greek-speaking part of the Roman empire; in the first century, one tetradrachm was equal to four drachmae or one denarius

tetrarch (*tet*-rark)

Greek for 'ruler of a quarter'; term for governor of part of a province in the Roman empire or a ruler of a minor principality

thalassa (*tha*-la-sa)

Greek word for 'sea'; this is what Xenophon and his men shouted after months of being lost inland and finally catching sight of water

Thebaid (thee-*bye*-id)

region of Upper Egypt around Thebes (modern Luxor and Karnak)

Titus (*tie*-tuss)

Titus Flavius Vespasianus, forty-one-year-old son of Vespasian, has been Emperor of Rome for almost a year when this story takes place

toga (*toe*-ga) a blanket-like outer garment, worn by free-born men and boys

triclinium (trik-*lin*-ee-um)

ancient Roman dining room, usually with three couches to recline on

tunic (*tew*-nik)

a piece of clothing like a big T-shirt; children often wore a long-sleeved one

tyche (*tie*-kee)

Greek word for 'luck' or 'fortune'

Tychicus (*tik*-ee-kuss)

early Christian who traveled with St Paul and is mentioned in some of his letters; we only know that he came from Ionia and ministered around Ephesus

Vespasian (vess-*pay*-zhun)

Roman emperor who ruled from AD 69–79; father of Titus and Domitian

vespasian (vess-*pay*-zhun)

slang term for 'piss-pot', so called because the emperor Vespasian had once set a tax on urine

Vesuvius (vuh-*soo*-vee-yus)

volcano near Naples which erupted on 24 August AD 79 and destroyed Pompeii

Via Ostiensis (*vee*-uh os-tee-*en*-suss)

road from Ostia to Rome

vinea (vin-*nay*-uh)

Latin for 'vineyard' or 'vines'

Virgo (*vur*-go)

Latin for 'virgin' or 'maiden'; sign of the zodiac of the maiden

Vulcan (*vul*-kan)

god of fire, the forge and blacksmiths

wall-nettle AKA herba murialis also known as parthenion, a herb recommended by Pliny and Celsus for bruises

wax tablet
a wax-covered rectanglar piece of wood used for making notes

wet-nurse
a woman who breast-feeds an infant if his mother is dead or can't feed him herself

Xenophon (*zen*-oh-fon)
(c.431–355 BC) a Greek who lived in the time of Plato; he led a group of mercenary soldiers who were lost for many months, when at last they caught sight of the sea, they knew they could find their way home to Greece

Yohanan (yo-*ha*-nan)
Hebrew for 'John'; John son of Zebedee was one of Jesus's disciples

Zabdai (*zab*-die)
Hebrew for 'Zebedee', a surname mentioned in the New Testament

Zodiac (*zo*-dee-ak)
Greek for 'animal figure': a belt of the heavens which includes twelve important constellations, (e.g. Virgo, the maiden); the ancients put great significance on the movement of the sun, moon and seven planets through these constellations

THE LAST SCROLL

Jesus of Nazareth was the name of the man who gave rise to the whole Christian faith. Some people believe he was the Son of God and that he performed miracles and rose from the dead. Others think he was just a wise prophet who lived in the first century AD. We know he was born about the year 'dot' and we still count our calendar from his birth. (AD stands for *anno domini* – 'in the year of the Lord' – and CE stands for 'Christian era'.) We know Jesus was Jewish, and that he spoke Aramaic and probably also Greek. We know that Jesus had at least a dozen disciples (all Jews) who followed him and claimed to have witnessed his miracles and resurrection. Almost all historians agree that Jesus was crucified in the Roman province of Judea around AD 30, during the reign of Tiberius, forty years before the destruction of Jerusalem by Titus's legions. We know that in the first century, Christianity seemed to be another sect of Judaism, and the two were often confused. Rome considered both dangerous because their followers would not worship deified Roman emperors, and this was considered subversive.

Apart from the New Testament, the part of the Bible that Christians use, there is good historical evidence for Jesus. He was mentioned by several first century Roman authors such as Pliny the Elder, Josephus, Tacitus and Suetonius. After his crucifixion, the disciples scattered to spread the good news about him: the 'gospel'. We do not have the same sort of historical evidence for them that we do for Jesus. However, tradition tells us that Peter went to Rome and was crucified near the spot in St Peter's Square where the obelisk now stands. Thomas went to spread the gospel in India, and James to Spain. There is also a tradition that James's brother John, 'the disciple Jesus loved', went to Ephesus with Mary the mother of Jesus and helped lead the lively churches in Asia Minor (modern Turkey). We call him John the Evangelist, to distinguish him from John the Baptist.

Some scholars believe John the Evangelist wrote one of the four gospels in the New Testament as well as some letters, and he may also have written the last book of the New Testament: the Book of Revelation. John called himself 'the disciple Jesus loved'. Tradition says he settled in Ephesus, and that he did not die until perhaps AD 100, seventy years after the crucifixion. If we assume he was in his early twenties when he became Jesus' disciple then this is perfectly possible. He would have been in his 70's when this story takes place and then he would have died in his nineties.

I have often wondered what might have happened if Flavia and her friends visited Ephesus and met St John or some other evangelists in AD 81. This story is the result of my imagining.

Tychicus is also mentioned in the New Testament. All we know is that he was a believer who preached around Ephesus. I have made up all the other details about him.